THE LAST DRAGON

A FOREST GUARDIANS NOVELLA

ALI INGS

ALI INGS

ISBN-13: 9781738061327
Cover design by: W. V. Rainy

CONTENTS

CHAPTER I

THE CHAMPION AND THE CHIEF

Her fingers tightened on the hilt of her sword. The worn leather compressed under her fingers. Her heart raced as metal struck metal. Light flashed; her shadowy hiding place was gone for the instant. The fireball spattered against the wood she ducked behind.

Ilia tugged on the worn leather strap holding her gorget in place. The leather neck protector was at least two sizes too big, but it was all she had. She peeked between the boards and into the arena. One knight was moving slower now, though his sword met each blow with a clash.

The smaller knight reached their arm out and grabbed the air, pulling back hard. The bigger knight landed on his back; his legs yanked by the spell. He hit with a grunt. A dust cloud rose, hiding him from sight. Ilia peered through the dust. Not even a glint from his shining armour was visible.

The smaller knight stepped into the dust and disappeared. The crowd was silent, waiting. The dust settled, falling slowly. The small knight stood over their opponent, their sword against his neck just below his helmet. The crowd burst into cheers and applause. Ilia waved her sword and hollered; her voice lost in the crowd.

The small knight pulled their helmet off and shook their long dark hair free. She met Ilia's gaze and smiled. Cheers erupted again as she raised her helmet in victory. She turned slowly around the arena, smiling and waving her helmet at the crowd, the slight breeze rustling her hair.

Ilia gripped her sword and dashed through the knights gathered along the arena edge with her. She pelted past the tents for the Knight-Mages, back to the training rings behind them. Apprentices and junior Knight-Mages filled most of the practice rings, training swords clashing as they practiced. Ilia took the smallest ring in the back, away from the others.

Her sword flashed as she swung it high and around. Now, down and back up, just like she did. Recover from his blow and a high strike to the head. What did she do next? Right, recover, and thrust. Ilia lunged, sword tip lashing out at where her opponent should be.

"That's good, but don't reach with your upper body. Lunge with a bigger step to close the distance. Your balance is more important than your reach."

Ilia's heartbeat pounded in her ears. The training grounds were silent, all eyes on the lady knight at the edge of Ilia's practise ring.

She spun and faced the knight, her fingers tightening on the sword hilt. She bowed her head. The leather gorget dug into her chin and pressed her neckband against her skin. "Thank you, Champion."

The woman laughed. "What do you call me in lessons?"

Ilia glanced up before dropping her gaze to the sand at her feet. "My apologies, Master."

The breeze picked up, blowing the woman's long dark hair into her face. She scowled and set her helmet on a post. She tossed her gauntlets aside and pulled a strip of green ribbon from under her armour. With deft fingers, the knight braided her hair. Her dusty hair hung neatly down her back, the ribbon braided in and holding it firm.

"This hair tie is amazing. It stays in place no matter what. Did you enchant it yourself?" The knight stepped beside Ilia and set a hand on the girl's shoulder.

Ilia barely felt the hand through the thick leather armour. "Yes, Master." She grinned up at her. "It was easy."

The knight smiled. "Now, I want to see that fighting set. Have you been practicing?" Those piercing violet eyes stared down at her. Through her, Ilia felt.

Ilia nodded. "Every chance I could. We've been busy in the Healing Wing with the knights needing help and all."

"Healing is your first responsibility, so never feel bad about putting it before sword practice. The world needs more healers and fewer reasons to fight. Show me what you've got."

The knight moved to the edge of the sand ring and leaned against the rough wooden boards. Ilia moved to the middle and closed her eyes. She took a slow breath. Her fingers ached as she gripped the sword. Would her legs hold her, or give out with how they shook? No, don't think about everyone watching. Just move.

Ilia drew her sword and struck out, lunging as far as her legs would take her. Don't lean, she reminded herself. Swing up and around, and smash down on my opponent. Ilia spun and twisted, stepped and slashed, stabbed and thrust. She panted as she spun and slashed before blocking and turning back to her starting position.

"Excellent." The lady knight walked to her side. "We have some things to work on, but you're doing well. Now, prepare yourself." She drew her sword and faced Ilia.

Ilia's eyes widened. Her arms shook as she raised her sword to the middle guard position. She stood frozen, her gaze on the woman's sword. No, on the woman, Ilia scolded herself. She shifted her focus to the knight.

The sword swung at her. Ilia raised her sword to a high block. Her arms vibrated as the swords clanged together. The knight shifted and Ilia reacted, swinging her sword down to guard her legs.

"Good. Keep going."

The sword swung at her ribs. Ilia charged forward and smashed the knight's armour-covered belly with her forearms. Her elbows ached at the impact, the leather arm protection barely softening the blow. The sword swung past behind her and the lady knight grunted.

Ilia bounced off and hit the dirt. Her helmet slid down over her eyes. Laughter rang out through the training grounds. Ilia's face burned, and she scowled at the sand.

Silence fell across the practice rings. A heavy rhythmic clinking caught Ilia's attention, coming closer. "Until you can see attacks coming that easily, you have no right to laugh." The deep voice had an edge like his sword, sharp, hard, and cold. "A knight doesn't laugh at others. A knight helps them up."

Ilia pushed herself to sit and shifted the helmet back from her eyes. Sunlight reflected off the metal gauntlet covering the massive hand before her. Ilia slid her small hand into his and the massive knight pulled her up. Her gaze followed the dusty armour up the muscular arm, past the heavy shoulder pauldrons, to the shining eyes of the massive knight. He smiled at her.

"Your idea was right, young one, but your execution needs work."

Ilia nodded. Her words were caught in her throat. He was big enough in the arena, but this close, he was absolutely huge. She didn't come up to his shoulder, but the lady knight didn't, either.

"For a push attack to work, you either need to be physically bigger, or magically rooted. You're small, but you're an Earth Mage. I can feel it. Can you root in the ground and hold yourself strong?"

Ilia nodded and took a breath. "We learn when we heal." I can also pull power right from the land, she added in her head, but I'm not about to mention that. Not again. People get so uncomfortable—

"Good. Try the move again, and this time root deep as you make impact. She knows it's coming, so you have to be strong and determined. We can do anything if we're determined enough."

The big knight stepped back and nodded at the lady knight. She shifted into a middle guard and waited for Ilia. The big knight picked up her sword and held it hilt out to her. Grains of sand bit into her unprotected hands as Ilia gripped her sword. She brought her sword up to the middle guard and waited.

The sword swung around at her ribs. Ilia brought her forearms up, her sword swinging over her shoulder, and charged. She touched the ground with her magical senses, reaching deep into the land below her. Ilia rooted herself magically and shoved, hitting the lady knight full force.

Her Master stumbled back, twisting and landing on one knee. She grinned up at Ilia. "That's it." Her voice was shaky, out of breath.

Ilia bowed her head and choked herself with her gorget. She lifted her chin and could breathe again. "I know you could have blocked it if you wanted," she whispered.

The lady knight stood and held her hand out to Ilia. "Yes, but you need a chance to try things and see how it works. That was powerful. No wonder you're the most promising Healer's Apprentice in the entire castle."

Ilia grasped the leather-wrapped hand and held it. "Thank you, Master."

"So, is this the mystery student you've been hiding from me?" The big knight laughed. "Has she had chances to spar with others yet?"

The lady knight smiled. "She has, but not as often as I'd like. Not all your troops are suitable for helping." She elbowed the massive knight in the side, just under his breastplate.

The big knight winced, his arm swinging down to hold his side. He scanned the training grounds, not scowling, but Ilia could see why nobody would meet his gaze. The place was full of knights and apprentices now, and they all suddenly looked incredibly busy. Where had they all come from? She listened but couldn't hear any cheering crowds. Were the matches done for the day?

"Any citizen who wishes to learn to defend themselves is to be given the opportunity if it does not clash with your own designated training or duties." His voice carried through the training grounds.

Ilia's cheeks burned. Sweat soaked her cotton robes under the heavy oversized leather armour she wore. The head of the King's Guard just gave her official permission to train openly. She and the Champion had been working for months, catching moments when she was back at the castle, but now Ilia could keep training when she was on missions, too.

He placed a hand on her shoulder and Ilia's knees buckled. "You may borrow anyone for her training who is available, and who you think is suitable." The big knight turned and strode from the ring.

"Like you could stop me," the lady knight teased.

He paused, glanced over his shoulder, smiled, and waved.

"You know him well?" Ilia watched the big man disappear into a tent.

The lady knight chuckled. "He was a constant thorn in my side during training. We became friends over time, and now we work together to keep everyone safe. It's a friendship of respect. Now I have time for a couple more rounds before I need to be presentable. Awards ceremonies and all."

Ilia laughed. She turned and faced her Master, her sword in the middle guard position. "I'm ready."

***

Ilia tugged at the strap behind her neck. Who thought putting the strap back there was a good idea? "These darned things are easier to get on than off," she mumbled.

"Here." Someone tugged at the strap and the gorget slipped loose.

"Thank you." Ilia took the gorget and set it on the armour mannequin. She turned and faced a young man in full metal plate armour. Where did she know him from? Ilia blushed. It was the massive knight's apprentice.

He smiled down at her. "Are you okay? Sometimes training sessions can take a lot out of us." He raised his eyebrow.

He's only a few years older than me, she realized. Ilia swallowed hard and nodded. "I'm fine, thanks," she whispered.

"Here. Allow me. It's good practice. Stand like this." He stood with his arms out at shoulder level, his legs spread to hip width. "It'll make this easier."

Please don't tremble, she pleaded to her body. Ilia shifted and held her arms out. The man gave her a kind smile. He had the palest yellow eyes she'd ever seen. His hands were smooth and fast as he unbuckled her armour, setting it on the mannequin with practiced motions.

"Doesn't he need you?"

The man chuckled. "I already got him presentable for the awards ceremony." He kneeled and unfastened the sabatons around her feet. "There. All done. Now, I'm betting you want to clean up before you go back to the Healing Wing."

Ilia narrowed her eyes at him, but kept her smile. "How did you know I was a healer?" Her light grey eyes held his gaze.

He rested his elbow on the mannequin and smiled. "I've seen you working with Master Silvan. Been in the Healing Wing a few times, myself, after training accidents. You've been there, helping out. My name is Eri."

Ilia smiled shyly, her gaze down at her dusty boots, before meeting his gaze again. "Ilia."

"Well, Ilia, it's a pleasure to meet you. Are you coming to the feast tonight?"

Ilia glanced down at her rumpled cotton robes and leggings. "If I get my work done, I'm sure Master Silvan will let me." She brushed her clothing smooth with her hands. "Oh." Ilia raised her wrist and looked at the red marks around it. The leather must have rubbed her, but how didn't she notice that?

"Adrenaline will do that." Eri nodded at her chafed wrist. "You'll feel it later if you don't heal it." He straightened and stepped closer. Eri took her wrist between warm hands. "I may not be a healer, but even I can fix that in no time. We get our share of minor injuries all the time."

Warmth flowed through her wrist and the slight burning eased. "Thanks. I better go. Master wanted my help this afternoon."

Eri bowed. "I'll see you at the feast."

Ilia grinned, her cheeks burning. "At the feast, then."

CHAPTER 2

HEALING MAGIC

Ilia muttered and passed her hand over her clothing. The dirt fell from her. Wrinkles disappeared from the cloth, leaving it smooth and dry, like they were newly laundered. Another quick spell and her skin and hair were clean. She'd need to change and shower before the feast. Magic could only do so much for hygiene, but it worked in a pinch.

She darted from the tent, dodging the knights in full metal armour at the entrance. Ilia crossed the training grounds and headed for the massive stone castle beyond them. The crowds had already gathered at the main ring for the awards ceremony, clearing her way to run for the main gate.

Guards on either side of the gate nodded to her as she tore through, heading for the open doors straight ahead of her. Once inside, she peeled off to the right and towards the archway to the Healing Wing. The banner hung over the entrance; gold embroidered potion bottles surrounded by the elemental symbols of each magic school. Healers came from all of them, though Water and Earth Mages were usually more gifted with healing.

She raced up the spiralling stone stairs to the second floor and down the hall to the far end. Her quarters were tidy and silent. Ilia glanced around. The potion station contained everything needed for brewing, already set up. Were they making potions this afternoon?

Master Silvan would be back soon enough. Ilia wandered to her bedroom. She took the advanced potions book from her desk and settled on her bed, reclining against the headboard. A Potion to Cure All Injury. Ilia read the recipe. Why hadn't anybody combined this with the previous recipe? She flipped back a page. The Potion for All Sickness. They shared so many ingredients already. If the two were combined, you'd have a magic cure-all for anything. Sure, it would need careful brewing and a new preservative, but the possibilities—

"Come, Child. Before you wander down and get distracted by the feast, we're going to do some work." Master Silvan leaned against her doorframe.

Ilia tucked the bookmark between the pages and set her book down. She stood and followed the older woman back into the main room.

Master Silvan walked to the large desk near the potions station. "It's time for you to make some charms on your own. I'll need a handful, and you're ready." She pulled a bag from over her shoulder and set it on the desk.

Ilia watched her pull materials from the bag, pieces of wood collected from the forest, thin twigs, horsehair from the stables, stones already shaped and polished, feathers from the rookery, and beads.

"I'll make one here while you watch. After that, you can make the rest."

Master Silvan sat in the chair and took a small circle of wood. She reached up and took a crystal from a ceramic box on the shelves above the desk, placing it in an earthenware holder. Ilia hadn't used fire crystals often, but she had a little experience.

"Burn this sigil into the wood." Her master gripped the earthenware holder like a quill, the crystal angled to the surface of the wood. "Press lightly, and let the crystal do the work."

Ilia wrinkled her nose at the burning smell. The wood blackened where the tip of the crystal had touched it, leaving a permanent mark on the light wood. Master Silvan worked with a steady hand and in moments, the symbol was complete.

"There are plenty more if you mess up and need to try again." Master Silvan gestured at the circles of wood, little cross-sections of a branch cut and shaped by Earth Magic. "Get it as close as possible, so it's effective."

Master Silvan stood and held the fire crystal out. Ilia slid into the chair and wrapped her fingers around the warm holder. The crystal glowed and pulsed with red light, sending warmth into the earthenware under her fingers.

"Now, we finish it like this."

Master Silvan picked up a strand of horsehair and some twigs. She bent them into shape and fastened them in place with the hair, adding beads and feathers as she worked. She added the sigil into the middle of the decorated twig wreath, tying it in place with another horsehair.

"Make five more just like this. Watch the placement and colour of the beads, mind, as it matters. I'll be brewing a potion right there, so if you have a question, just ask."

"Yes, Master."

Ilia took a circle of wood and set the crystal on the surface. Her hand was steady, and she copied the symbol exactly. Her second try was not so successful. The burning smell made her sneeze and her hand wobbled. She tossed the wood aside and took another. Soon enough she had all five sigils done, and only a couple of ruined attempts. All that time she spent practicing copying as a student paid off. Ilia smiled widely.

Master Silvan glanced over. She nodded. "Good work. I'll show you how to dispose of the ruined ones later."

Ilia picked up a strand of horsehair. She selected twigs and bent them into shape. The wood was flexible, and she added a touch of Earth Magic when needed to get the shape perfect. "What's this charm for? It's full of healing symbols, but I've never seen this sigil before."

Lavender scent drifted through the room as Master Silvan crushed the flowers in the Mortar and Pestle. "Some knights have an infection I've never seen before. This charm is stopping it from spreading while we find a cure. I'm brewing a new potion we hope will work." The metal ladle clanged against the side of the cauldron.

Ilia nodded and got back to work. If the potion worked, she'd get a chance to try brewing it later. The biggest benefit to being a Master Healer's apprentice, aside from her own quiet room, was getting to learn all about the new potions before the other students. She even helped make a few in these last few years.

Focus, she reminded herself. Ilia pulled a bead back off the hair and tied a twig in place before adding the bead where it belonged.

"Mind you get an exact match."

Ilia grit her teeth. She took a slow breath and let it out as she rolled her shoulders.

"I know. I'm sorry. I was just supervising the third-year students, and old habits are hard to break." Master Silvan added a powder, and the potion foamed and turned blue.

Ilia slipped the last knot in place and glanced at her master.

The old woman smiled, a rare thing, in Ilia's experience. "You know what you're doing. Carry on."

***

Ilia set the last charm on the desk. She leaned back against the chair and stretched her arms over her head. Master Silvan poured the potion into small vials. Ilia slipped from her chair and walked over. She pulled the candle from the shelf and set it on the worktable nearby. A quick muttered spell, a waved hand, and a little flame flickered to life.

"Thanks, Child. Seal these, and we'll go to the main potion lab to finish. There's one more to brew, and we'll want help to get enough."

Ilia picked up a little vial Master Silvan had corked, and she dripped wax around the edges. Ilia could feel the sigil for preservation carved into the candle as she held it over the vials, one at a time. Spices released into the air as the candle burned, filling the room with a sweet fragrance. Her stomach growled.

Master Silvan smiled. "We'll be done soon. You can enjoy that feast and even some dancing, as long as you're in bed by midnight. We have morning shift, so don't forget."

Ilia ducked her head and hid her grin. "I won't forget."
Morning shift meant helping directly with patients and
doing the morning rounds with the full healers. There's
no way she was going to miss that.

"Now, the basket, Child. Let's finish up. I want to feast,
too."

She pulled a basket from under the worktable and packed
the little vials inside. Master Silvan added bottles of dried
herbs from her private cupboard as well. The old woman
picked up the basket and nodded. Ilia followed her down
the stairs to the main floor and into the nearby main potion lab.

Ilia loved the soft bubbling sound of potions simmering.
Cauldrons sat at each workstation, with more sizes on the
shelves below the tabletops. Ingredients lined shelves and
filled cupboards, all carefully inventoried and ready for
use. Bottles and packages and baskets of ingredients had a
label in a neat script identifying the contents.

Master Silvan marched to the frontmost worktable and set
the basket down. "Advanced students, come to the front
stations. Herbalists, prepare your workstations. We have
some brewing to do." She rubbed her hands together and
looked over the mages in the room.

Ilia walked to the side workstations with the trained and
certified herbalists. She ran her fingers over the smooth
tabletop, worn and polished from use. While she still had
so much to learn, she got her certification a while ago. Ilia

smiled at the memory, right here at this very workstation. She traced her carved initials on the side, done long ago in an early potion lesson.

"We're doing the Potion of Protection. Use formula four, with no deviations. Gather your supplies and begin. Ask if you have any questions, and don't be afraid to get help from an herbalist, students. Additional ingredients are here." Master Silvan gestured at the bottles she pulled from her basket and set on her workstation.

Ilia gathered the ingredients from the various shelves and set them on her workstation. She filled her cauldron part way with water and coaxed the fire into life in the firebox below it. A touch of magic and the fire burned hot, boiling her water for her. While she waited, Ilia measured out the specific ingredients and set them in little bowls, ready to dump into the cauldron when it was time.

There, a gentle simmer now. Ilia reduced the fire with her magic. First, the powdered flowers. Ilia tipped the little dish over the cauldron and tapped the edge, sprinkling the powder inside. She tapped the dish one last time, getting every last speck of powder in.

Her chest ached. It felt like someone was trying to turn her inside out. She gripped the robes over her heart, her fingers growing pale. Ilia gasped for breath. She grabbed for the tabletop as her legs gave out. Her hand hit the scales as she slid to the floor. The metal scales tumbled to the floor beside her with a crash.

"Who made all the—Ilia! Are you alright?"

She could barely hear Master Silvan, her words jumbled together and almost indistinct. Blood rushed through her ears, the pounding of her heart louder than her surroundings. Pain flooded through her, worse than anything she felt before. Make it stop. Please, make it stop.

Icy fingers pressed against her forehead. Comfort poured into her like a warm blanket on a wintry day. Her shaking stopped. Her stomach calmed, though her heart still ached. Ilia wiped her forehead with the sleeve of her soft robes and blinked up at Master Silvan.

"Sit, Child." Her master helped her sit propped up against the workstation. "What happened?" Master Silvan peered into her eyes.

"I felt—" Ilia stared at the stone floor. "It felt like the magic was being sucked from me."

Master Silvan ignored the powders on the floor and shoved the scales aside as she kneeled beside Ilia. "How do you feel now?" She took Ilia's hands and held them firmly. "Any change in your powers?"

Ilia took a slow breath and felt inside. The magic swirled inside her still, no longer pooled in her belly, but up near her heart and lungs. It was as strong as ever, though. "I think I'm okay. What did I feel?"

"Did anyone else feel anything?" Master Silvan stood and stared around the room, holding everyone's eye contact in turn.

Ilia heard the chorus of "no" or "no, Ma'am."

"Finish your potions. Menin, you're in charge." Master Silvan eased an arm around Ilia and helped her stand. "Come, Child. You need a drink, and I want a better look at you."

Her legs shook, and she clutched the workstation to steady herself. Now that the pain eased, she felt a stabbing pain in her side, but more like a memory than an actual injury. It went straight through her ribs to her heart. Ilia brushed her fingers over the spot, but her body felt normal.

Master Silvan walked her through her spilled ingredients and across the workroom, one slow step at a time. For an old woman, she has an iron grip. What happened, though?

They passed through the curtained doorway and into the main Healing Wing. Ilia glanced at the treatment rooms they passed, each with a man or woman laying on a bed, most wrapped in bandages.

"What happened to them?" Ilia whispered.

Master Silvan glanced into the next room they passed. She looked down at Ilia for a long moment as she led the girl into the next treatment room. "Have a seat. I'm going to do a thorough check here, where there's privacy."

ALI INGS

Wasn't she going to answer?

CHAPTER 3

WHAT HAPPENED?

"They were in the mountains to the southeast, on a special mission for the king. That's all I can say."

Ilia eased herself to the bed. Her legs gave out part way down and she collapsed on the mattress. "They look like they've been in battle." She pushed herself back up to sit on the edge of the bed.

"They were. That's not your concern now, though. You can learn more when we do rounds tomorrow." Master Silvan took Ilia's hands.

Ilia smiled and relaxed. As worried as she was, Master Silvan still treated her normally. Whatever was wrong, it couldn't be that serious. "I still get to do rounds with you?"

"You've earned it, Child. You're a natural at healing, and you're ready to move to the next stage of training. Now, sit quietly and let me do this."

Ilia twitched and shifted. Master Silvan narrowed her eyes at the girl, and she went still. Ilia closed her eyes and slowed her breathing. Calm. A healer must be calm. Patients can heal themselves if we're calm and believe they will, and that takes control.

"Better, Child. Your magic feels fine to me. What happened?" Master Silvan pulled a stool from the corner of the small room and sat facing Ilia.

Ilia shrugged. "I don't know. I felt fine. The powder was pouring perfectly for me. The next thing I knew, I felt like I was being thrust through with a sword. My ribs wanted to explode, and my heart ached. I couldn't breathe."

Master Silvan got up and stepped to the cupboard. She retrieved a bottle and uncorked it. A nerve tonic? No, there was a ring of gold liquid at the top. What's that potion for? How do the many parts of the potion stay separate? Ilia raised an eyebrow.

"Drink it all, Child. I know it's a lot, but you need it. This potion protects against magical interference." Master Silvan held the bottle out to her.

The delicate scent of Nordomine blossoms wafted up to her, sweet and floral. Cinnamon? Something else, a light oil of some kind. Coconut oil. Ilia smiled. She took the bottle and tipped it against her lips, taking a large mouthful. Ilia choked, and the bottle slipped from her hands. Master Silvan caught the bottle and held it up for her as Ilia sputtered and coughed.

"Ugh." Ilia wiped her mouth with her sleeve. Her robes definitely needed laundering now. "Salty."

"The salt is protective. Drink it all, and you can have as much water as you want when you're done."

Ilia gulped down the potion, trying not to taste it. She shifted onto the bed, leaning back against the headboard, and wrapped her arms around her belly.

"Here. It'll help." Master Silvan took a massive glass from the cupboard and filled it with a pipe at the counter.

Water flowed into the glass, stopping when it was nearly full. She handed the glass to Ilia, and the girl gulped it down in a few big swallows, despite the amount. As promised, the water cleared the salt from her mouth.

"Rest. They'll clean up for you. Don't leave this room until I say so. I'll be back soon."

Master Silvan set the water glass on the counter. She opened another cupboard and pulled out some crystals. She set one in each corner of the room.

"I call on the power entrusted to you, protect and guard those inside, through and through. Let no other powers inside. Guard her, protect her, in peace she'll reside." Her voice was steady through the chant.

The crystals glowed with a pale white light. A wreath hung above the door, and a crystal within the branches glowed as well.

"Stay here, Child. I'll be back soon." Master Silvan left the room, closing the door behind her.

Ilia glanced around the room. It was so quiet, like all life had been banished or something. Only the sound of her own breathing kept her company. The room was small, holding the bed and a small night table, the stool, and the cupboards along one wall.

She leaned closer to the nearest crystal and peered at it. Were those tiny threads of light flowing between the crystals? She hadn't started crystal magic yet, though she'd read a little about it. Usually, it was only used when facing evil, often as a small stone carried in the pocket or in jewelry. Encasing a room in protection? Was she in danger?

Why did she need protection from magical interference? Who would care about a girl in the castle, just one of many, and an apprentice healer without parents, at that? What could they hope to gain? Ilia wiggled under the blanket and snuggled into the warmth. Her head hit the pillow and her eyes closed. The crystals glowed steadily, spots of light visible through her eyelids.

***

"Wake up, Ilia."

A hand shook her shoulder, pulling her from sleep. Ilia batted at the hand and rolled over. She was warm and comfortable and finally stopped hurting.

"You've been summoned."

Her eyes popped open. "Summoned?" She rolled back over and stared up into Master Healer Damian's eyes. "Whatever for?" She sat, letting the blankets fall away.

The small man shrugged, his light brown hair flopping over the left side of his face as he tilted his head. "Master Silvan is already there with the advisors, and they're waiting for you. Come. I'll escort you there." He picked up the crystal from the night table and dropped it into a fine metallic net bag. "Wear this around your neck. Keep it with you until Master Silvan says otherwise."

Ilia took the thin silver chain and held it up. The crystal hung in the little metal net, secure and safe, and still glowing. It was far heavier than she expected. Ilia ducked her head and dropped the chain over it, letting the crystal settle over her chest.

"Tuck that under your robes. Let's go."

Ilia slipped the crystal under her robes and shifted from the bed. At least her legs were holding her this time. Master

Damian led her through the door and into the hall. Ilia hustled to keep up. He led her the most direct route to the Main Hall, passing easily through the crowded main entryway.

The massive doors into the Main Hall stood closed. Master Healer Damian headed for a small door set within a larger door. Ilia squirmed as she approached the towering doors, wide enough for eight people to walk abreast when open. The oiled wood shone in the mage-light.

"Go on in." Master Healer Damian opened the door and stepped aside.

Ilia stared at the opening. Should she really be here?

"This way, Miss." A guard on the other side waved for her to join him.

Ilia walked through and followed the guard along the edge of the hall. Another guard at the door watched her go. Ilia took a steadying breath and walked as tall as she could. The guard's armour reflected the mage-light as they passed under sconces. He led her to near the throne, where Master Silvan waited for her. Once Ilia was at her side, the Knight-Mage bowed his head and left, returning to his post at the doors.

"Your Highness, I saw it with my own eyes."

Ilia stayed behind Master Silvan, barely able to see through the advisors standing with her. She glimpsed a

Knight-Mage kneeling on the floor, his armour stained with blood and dust. Even with his helmet off, she couldn't tell hair colour through the grime.

The door opened and two more mages came in, wearing the robes of advisors. They joined Ilia's group near the throne.

"Now that everyone is here, tell the court again what you saw and experienced." The king sat upon the dais on his throne. His golden jewelry gleamed in the mage-light lamps. No, not jewelry, Ilia reminded herself, artifacts. Magical power, stored in items he could wear on his person.

"We got to the pass as ordered. We were too late. The dragon lay on a rock, a lance through its heart. There was no sign of the mate anywhere. A dozen mages were around the body, stripping it of scales and shaping it into armour. Your Highness, there are two Dark Knights roaming the land now."

The King stared down at the kneeling Knight-Mage. "Advisors, your thoughts?" He rubbed his greying beard.

"Your Highness, this is grave news indeed." Master Seer Forda stepped forward. "The dragon population is already at critically low levels. We need to protect any that are left. If the dragons disappear, we don't know what that will do to the magic in this land. It could disappear as well."

Gasps and mutters broke through the silence. Voices rose.

"Silence," the King commanded, his voice drowning out the murmurs and noise.

Nobody moved. Was anybody breathing? It was so quiet, Ilia barely dared to exist.

"Is anyone alive still who has beaten a Dark Knight before? Anyone at all, no matter how old?" The King turned his piercing gaze on the advisors.

Ilia shifted behind Master Silvan, out of his sight.

"Highness, the records and legends both show White Knights can defeat a Dark Knight." Master Librarian Dinoc stepped forward.

"Find one. Bring them to me."

Master Dinoc stared up for a moment before bowing his head. "As I was about to say," he stammered, "the last one died just under a century ago. For a White Knight to rise, a dragon must willingly give up their scales and shape the armour for the knight. If a dragon loses their scales, they die."

The King frowned. His stare was as cold as ice. "How many dragons are left?"

"We don't know. We'll have to go look. Not many. We need time to find answers." Master Dinoc twisted his fingers together behind his back. His hands were nearly white.

"Highness." Master Silvan stepped forward, dragging Ilia with her by the robes. "My apprentice felt the dragon die."

Everyone turned their gaze on Ilia. She inched closer to Master Silvan.

"Is this true, girl?" The King's copper-coloured eyes fixed on hers, daring her to lie, it felt.

"I don't—I don't know what I felt," Ilia managed, her voice shaking as bad as her legs. "It hurt, though." She rubbed her ribs where the lingering memory of pain remained.

"Is she tied to the dragons somehow? Who are her parents? What is her magic?" The King gazed down at her neckband.

Ilia's hand moved up to her neck, her fingers running over the silver neckband and the clusters of crystals, three emerald crystals and a light blue one in each grouping.

"Highness, she's an orphan. I've raised her since she was a baby." Master Silvan squeezed Ilia's shoulder. "I don't know fully what she's capable of. Every time I try and see her future, I see only white light."

"You all have until morning to find answers. Go."

Mages scattered. Master Silvan steered Ilia from the room by her arm, out a side door and into the Advisor's Meeting Room. She marched Ilia through the quieter back halls and into the Healing Wing, back to the small room with

31

the crystals. Ilia collapsed on the bed and held her ribs, the muscles aching.

"Sit here, Child, and wait." Master Silvan moved to the cupboard and pulled out a locked chest.

Ilia shifted and leaned, trying to see into the chest from the bed, but she couldn't. It was too high. Master Silvan took another crystal and set it on the night table, restoring the magical protection for Ilia. The old woman returned and retrieved a charm, a little metal medallion on a finely braided chain.

"Wear this, Child. Don't take that crystal off. Wear them both. They'll work together to give you more protection. Don't remove either until I tell you it is safe."

Ilia slipped the chain over her head. She picked up the little charm. It was a filigreed tree with tiny emeralds where the leaves would be. Ilia tucked the charm under her shirt.

"Now, stay here and rest. Don't leave the room without permission."

Ilia closed her eyes and her chin dropped to her chest.

Master Silvan set a hand on her shoulder. "I'll have a plate brought for you, full of delights, including some pastries. I'm sorry you'll miss the feast."

Ilia managed a shaky smile. "Thank you."

CHAPTER 4

WHAT TO DO?

I lia blinked. The room was dark, except for the soft glow of the crystals. She wrinkled her nose at the medicinal smell even the flowers and herbs couldn't quite cover. Where was she? Right, a treatment room.

Muffled voices grabbed her attention, somewhere just outside her door. Ilia strained her ears to make out any words.

"The girl felt—dragon—means—she—save us."

Ilia sat bolt upright. She smoothed her wild and curly brown hair down. Ilia straightened her hair tie and slipped from the bed. Master Silvan just might kill her herself if Ilia left the room, but she didn't say anything about leaving the bed. Ilia crept to the door and sat, hoping to hear better through the gap at the bottom.

"She's a child. A student, still. I don't care if she can save the Universe, she's not going out there into the wild, dragon or no."

Ilia raised her eyebrow. Into the wild?

"She can feel dragons, Meretha. She can find them faster than we can once she's shown how. We have to scry for them, and they sometimes shield themselves, or we must go out and look. She might just know, just by feeling for them."

Feel dragons? She rubbed her ribs. The only time she felt a dragon, Ilia thought she was going to die. She'd never done it before and had no idea how to try again. How did Master Dinoc know she even could? Sure, she had talent with potions, and sometimes saw images in wash buckets, but that's it.

"You want a child to look for dragons? With Dark Knights roaming the land? What happens if they find her? You know how fast rumors spread. There were some big mouths at the meeting yesterday. They might already be on their way to kidnap her. If she can feel dragons for us, what makes you think they won't want her?"

Ilia clutched the crystal in her hand through her thin cotton night robe. The chain pulled against her neck, digging in above her neckband. Kidnapped? Here, in the castle? Surely, she was safe here, right?

"She wouldn't be alone. Knight-Mages would go with her. She'd be fine."

"Like the knights laying in these beds are fine?"

Ilia drew back. She'd never heard Master Silvan so upset.

"She could help save us all. Do you want magic to disappear, and with it, our entire way of life? How many people might die if you don't have magic to heal them?"

Ilia blinked. Had Master Dinoc ever raised his voice before? He always spoke in the hushed tones of a librarian.

"She's a child, and she's staying here. The matter is closed. Now, get out. You're disturbing the patients."

Footsteps approached her door. Ilia darted to the bed and threw herself on it, rolling under the covers as the door opened a crack. A sliver of light crossed her bed. Ilia closed her eyes and lay as still as she could. The light disappeared, and the latch clicked shut. Footsteps faded.

Ilia rolled and smoothed her blankets. She pulled them over herself fully and snuggled into the warmth. Could she feel dragons? She never tried before. Magic starts within, in our pool of power down in the belly. She still remembered that lecture after all these years.

She slowed her breathing and focused inside. Her power swirled and churned inside. She felt the bedframe and the wooden cupboards, the door, her blankets, even the air currents in the room. No dragons, though. Master Dinoc must be wrong.

Ilia blinked and opened her eyes. She stretched. Her senses returned to normal, the feel of nature around her fading away. No one else felt their surroundings like she could. When she mentioned it, people thought she was crazy. Only Master Silvan listened with interest.

What if she could help, though? What if she could save everyone all at once? Would she? Could she? What if Master Dinoc is wrong and she can't sense the dragons?

Her brain ached. She needed sleep. Ilia rubbed her temples and took another slow breath. Maybe she'd find a book in the library that could help her. She'd look as soon as she could leave the room without risking death.

***

Ropes wound tightly around her. Ilia struggled to pull in a breath. The rough fibers cut into her and held snug. Ilia toppled to the floor, her head aching with the impact. Screaming filled the air. Her ears ached, and she couldn't cover them. Heat rolled past her as a fireball shot over her.

Sweat beaded on her skin. The salt burned where the ropes cut in. Ilia squeezed her eyes shut. Breathe slowly, she reminded herself. Manage the pain. She focused on the ropes as she called on her Earth Magic.

Clink. Clink. Clink. Footsteps approached; feet encased in armour. A black gauntleted hand grasped her hair and pulled her head around. Ilia fought the ropes, wriggling to free herself. Her skin burned.

She bolted up, her hands gripping the bedsheets. Sweat soaked through her robes. The sheets tangled around her, squeezing her tightly. She wrapped her hand around the crystal, still around her neck, and her panic eased. Her heart slowed and she could breathe again. Just a dream, but it felt so real.

That hallway, that stone floor in her dream, it was right outside her door. She recognized the screams, knew the people who were dying in her dream. Wait, they're all safe. Everyone is safe. It was just a dream.

Was it, though? She saw things on reflective surfaces sometimes. Those things happened within a week, usually. No, this had to be a dream, nothing more.

Were the walls closing in? Ilia pulled at her cotton robes. Fresh air, that's what she needs. Ilia glanced at the crystals. She'd be scrubbing cauldrons and bedpans for a decade if she left the room without permission. Her hands shook.

Ilia pulled back the covers and slipped from the bed. The forest was calling, and Ilia needed to see the stars. Things always seemed more clear in the woods when she had time alone with her thoughts. She wobbled a few steps and stopped at the door.

Light flowed through under the crack at the bottom. No talking, no footsteps, not a sound reached her ears. Ilia was alone. She eased the door open a crack and listened again. Still nothing. Ilia slipped through the door and crept down the hallway.

She peeked around the corner. A healer sat at a desk, his back to her, his attention on something in front of him. Ilia crept past, down another hall. Her door to freedom was ahead. She gripped the metal handle and turned it; her small fingers wrapped around the thick iron. The heavy latch clicked and released. Ilia smiled. Whatever magic made the doors recognize castle residents, she was grateful for it.

CHAPTER 5

INTO THE WOODS

I lia stepped out into the warm night breeze and closed the door behind her. The grass tickled her feet as she crossed the wide lawn, the soil soft beneath her cushioning each step. Her body relaxed, and she sighed. The forest was close, and she was safe.

She crossed the grass and wandered into the forest, each tree a tall sentinel on guard, protecting the smaller plants and the animals within. An owl flew past over her head. The breeze from his wings ruffled her hair. It hooted.

"Hello, little friend. It's nice to see you, too," she whispered.

Her power swirled inside her, awake within her among the trees like this. Ilia closed her eyes and opened her other senses to the forest. Each tree and plant responded to her magic, resonating in a shared energy. She felt them all around her, an awareness of where they were and how healthy each plant was.

She opened her eyes and walked among the trees. Moonlight shone down on the river, the light sparkling on the rippling water. The break in the trees exposed the night sky to her, each star shimmering overhead. Ilia turned and glanced up at the tower behind her, where the official astronomers worked. The view from up there was amazing, though she didn't get to see it often enough.

Ilia sank to the soft grass beside the river. She leaned over the water and watched the reflected stars dance on the rippling surface. Ilia dipped her fingers into the water. The current pulled on her hand, cold and strong, numbing her skin in moments.

With closed eyes, Ilia felt around herself again. The river burst with life, algae and water plants clinging to the rocks, especially in pools and eddies. Plants grew strong with steady access to water like this. Ilia opened her eyes and glanced around at the forest, lighted by the nearly full moon. Even under the canopy of leaves, she saw well enough to run if she needed. Ilia shivered at the thought. No, there was nothing out here, just her forest and the animals within it.

Something tugged at her senses, a wrongness she couldn't quite name. Ilia closed her eyes and felt again. Where was it? What was it? She opened her eyes and peered into the shadows. No, it was too far. She just couldn't see anything. Ilia closed her eyes and felt again.

Like a man, it walked upright. It was like a shadow in her senses, not something she felt directly, but something she knew about because it blurred out the life around it. It's like there was no energy there at all. She opened her eyes and strained to see whatever approached her like a shadow.

Something moved at the edge of the trees, just across the river from her. A shadow was blacker than normal. Her heart hammered against her ribs. Light reflected off the blackness, almost an iridescent shine. Her stomach flopped, and she suppressed the urge to be sick.

Ilia leapt to her feet and ran. No, not for the castle. Not that hallway, and not where my friends might die. She turned and ran south, deep into the forest and away from those she cared about. Was it coming for her? Her legs pumped, and she ran as fast as she could, not looking back.

She darted among the trees, from shadow to shadow. The bright moonlight filtered through the leaves, speckling the ground below her feet. She dodged bushes and leapt fallen logs as she ran, pelting headlong into the forest.

Her chest heaved and her legs burned as they gave out. Dirt sprayed up around her as she tumbled to the grass. Soil clung to her pale grey night robes. She rested her chin on her hand and focused on slowing her breathing. Her pulse pounding in her ears drowned out the forest noises. No, she needed to listen and feel.

Ilia closed her eyes and counted as she breathed, calming her body with each exhale. Now, try again. Feel. Where is it?

Night sounds surrounded her, birds and owls active as they hunted, the leaves rustling gently in the breeze, the forest as it should be. Animals greeted or ignored Ilia, instead of fleeing from her presence like they usually did around people. A few smaller birds twittered to each other in a nearby tree. She must be alone.

There were no footsteps, no clinking of armour, no sounds of another person nearby. Did she outrun it? How big was her head start? Was it even following, or was it in the castle, attacking her friends without her? The urge to go back filled her, pulled and called to her. Ilia gripped the grass beneath her hands and took a slow breath. No, she wasn't going back, just in case it was following her.

She rolled over and scooted closer to the nearest tree. Leaning back against the rough trunk, she stared up through the leaves at a small patch of sky. Was it just a dream or was it a premonition? What was that thing? Who could she ask? Master Silvan was back at the castle, the one place she dared not go. Who else knew about these things?

Her throat felt dry. Ilia needed water. She closed her eyes and felt around. She licked her dry lips. How long had she run for? After all her training runs with the Champion, she still couldn't estimate distances the way that woman could. The moon was dropping, and faint golds and purples of sunrise were just appearing.

Ilia smiled. There was a stream nearby. She eased herself up and followed the sensation. It wasn't long before she heard the trickle of running water. Ilia followed the sound. She opened herself and let her magical senses out again. Animals were quiet, going about their foraging or resting in burrows. She didn't sense them directly but felt them as they climbed the trees or curled up among the leaves.

She dropped to her knees beside the water and scooped some up in her hand. Ilia drank her fill, the cold making her teeth ache, but she didn't care. With her thirst taken care of, Ilia felt about for food. She hunted under the shrubs at the water's edge, exposing small plants with tender white flowers. Ilia picked the plants and ate, flowers and all.

Ilia settled down between some trees, curled up among the bushes, and closed her eyes.

***

She gasped. The cold water dripped from her face and off her fingers. Oh, how she missed those leisurely wake-ups in the castle, under warm blankets, with the smell of fresh tea to entice her from bed. No, a quick cold-water wash was the best she'd get here.

Ilia looked around. Now, where was she? She'd never come this far south before. Was she still south, or had she turned around in the night, during her wild flight? She could see the sun, up through the leaves above her, so she knew what direction she faced, but what direction had she gone?

Within minutes, Ilia gathered plenty of berries, herbs, and roots for breakfast. A touch of Earth Magic and digging roots was a breeze. Ilia smiled. With her Air Magic, a breeze was pretty easy, anyway. She shook her head. No time for bad mage humour. She needed to figure out where she was.

She picked up a root, and the dirt fell away, courtesy of a little magic. They tasted better cooked, but the roots were safe to eat raw. She munched on her meal as she scanned the surrounding forest, naming all the plants she could.

A twig snapped. Ilia spun towards the sound. Her heart raced. Abandoning her breakfast, Ilia snuck into the bushes. She pressed herself low to the ground. Please, hide me, forest, she pleaded.

Boots appeared near her breakfast, a sturdy brown leather covering enormous feet. A second pair of boots followed behind, appearing moments later.

"I was sure I heard something." A young man, from the sound of it.

Ilia wrinkled her brow. The voice was familiar, wasn't it?

"Things that hide, concealed from me, reveal yourself and let me see," a deep voice chanted, so softly Ilia barely made out the words.

Please, forest, she pleaded again. Don't let them find me. I can't go back until I have answers.

"Nothing. Could we be mistaken, or are they shielded somehow?" The younger man kneeled beside her abandoned breakfast and picked up a piece of her root. "Animals, you think?"

Did she dare move a few leaves and see who it was? Would they spot her if she did?

"No. Animals would take that back to their dens or nests, not leave it behind in neat piles. See the tracks? Whoever it was came and stopped right here. They're probably not far. Look around."

The feet separated, each man going different directions. Ilia counted her breathing, forcing herself to remain still under the bushes. How long would they look? The massive boots walked away. The younger man circled her bushes, going wide around her trees.

Please leave, she pleaded in her head.

"I don't see anyone." The smaller boots stopped at her breakfast.

The massive boots reappeared in her sight from a completely different direction. She didn't even hear him walk.

He just seemed to be there suddenly. "Come. We keep moving."

The men walked off together, towards where she thought she came from. Ilia rolled her shoulders slowly, easing the tension from laying on the ground hunched up. Were they headed to the castle? Could she follow them at a distance? It was one thing to sneak about a castle. Ilia was an expert at that, but she had no experience being sneaky in the forest. No, she can't go back, she reminded herself. She needs help.

Ilia took some slow breaths, her fingers gripping her leggings and turning white. They had to be gone by now, right? Had it been seconds or minutes? The chief astrologer showed her how to estimate the time of day by the sun, but she couldn't count minutes off with it.

Ilia crept from her bushes and looked around. She couldn't see or hear anyone nearby. She stood and looked again. They must be gone. With a smile on her face, Ilia turned west and took a confident step.

Thank the Spirits I got—the ground disappeared under her as she swung up into the trees. She hung beside the tree trunk, surrounded by a net of moss and vines. Ilia pushed against the cords of plants. They felt like regular rope, flexible and strong. Ilia peered down at the ground below her. The soil had scuffmarks from where the net lay waiting for her, hidden in the grass.

Could she climb out? Ilia gripped the vines and stood, the net swaying with each movement. The top was closed together with magic, sealing her inside. She pulled at the vines, but the openings were too small to wriggle through.

Damp with sweat and heart racing, Ilia slumped down in the net. Her chest muscles ached from breathing hard and fighting the net. A tear rolled down her cheek. She closed her eyes and curled up. The net swayed gently, like a rocking chair.

"Ilia? What are you doing out here?"

Her eyes snapped open. She recognized the voice. Ilia wriggled around. "Eri?" Thank the Spirits, it's someone she knows.

The massive knight stepped beside her. He reached out and pulled her and the net into his arms. His fingers snapped, and the net dissolved around her, the plants dropping back to the soil they came from. "What are you doing out here, young one?" The emerald crystals shone in his platinum neckband. She saw it clearly being held like that.

Ilia closed her eyes, the bright green of the crystals still in her mind. What could she tell him? "I wanted some air after a nightmare. I got turned around in the dark and got lost."

"We'll take you back." The massive knight set her down, her feet touching the ground lightly.

"If you point me in the right direction, I can make it back in the light." *I'll slip away once you're gone and continue on my way,* she added to herself.

"But, Master, what about our mission?" Eri glanced to the southwest.

CHAPTER 6

OUT IN THE WORLD

The big man frowned; his arms folded over his chest as he looked down at Ilia. Ilia dropped her gaze to her bare feet, glanced over at a bush, watched her fingers twist around together in front of her, looked up at a bird flittering between the trees—

"We can't just let her wander. She got lost, and it can happen again."

Ilia turned her pleading gaze on him. "Please, Sir. In the light, I'll be fine. I can't have gone far." Please work, she pleaded. Don't take me back.

"Ilia, we're miles from the castle." Eri raised an eyebrow.

"You'll come with us. We're heading to Mithlan. I can arrange a wagon ride back for you from there."

Ilia opened her mouth. The knight stared down at her, an arched eyebrow daring her to speak. Ilia closed her mouth.

She wasn't going back right away, at least. Besides, this was her chance to see more of the country.

The knight set his pack on the ground and pulled out a self-inking quill and parchment. He scratched a note and folded it up, little wings extending from the shape he made. He tossed the note in the air and the tiny wings flapped. It zipped off towards the castle.

"Are you warm enough?" Eri glanced down at her bare feet.

Ilia shivered, unable to suppress it.

"The pack." The big knight gestured at Eri.

The young man turned, and the knight stepped behind him. He went through the pack and pulled a tunic from the main compartment. Wordlessly, he handed it to Ilia. She took the soft cloth in her hands.

He waved a hand over her and chanted. "There. We'll turn and you can change. Don't try to run. The circle will contain you."

They turned so their backs were to her. She held the thick wool tunic between her knees and wriggled her sweaty cotton night robes off. Her skin prickled in the cool morning air. Ilia eased the woolen tunic over her head and let it drop over her body. It was huge on her, with room for a few more of her inside, but she was warm again. It covered her almost to her ankles. Fortunately, the side slits would let her walk easily, while keeping her covered.

"Thank you." Ilia bundled her night robes and held them to her body.

The big knight held his hand out and she passed him the robes. He tucked them in the pack. "I don't have boots your size, or even close enough to be magicked."

"I'll be fine." Ilia smiled up at him. "I walk barefoot while gathering herbs all the time." It lets me feel the soil and know where the plants are better, she added to herself. Then again, he's an Earth Mage. He might understand. Might.

"Come. Let us know if you get tired or have any problems." The big knight turned and started walking. He waved for her to catch up.

She sighed. Maybe in Mithlan she could find someone who knew about premonitions. It was a big city, supposedly, and she might be able to slip away. Maybe there would be a way to contact Master Silvan and ask her? No, she'd be furious if Ilia left. She'd figure something out and find someone to ask.

Ilia darted up beside the big knight. She fell into step beside him. Eri walked on her other side. Ilia glanced up at Eri. Dark blue crystals glittered in his silver neckband. He was still a student, like her. She smiled. Water Mages and Earth Mages often got along incredibly well. No wonder she felt so relaxed around him. Water Mages made excellent healers, but had she ever seen a knight with Water Magic? Ilia got lost in her memories in the training yards.

Eri glanced down at her. "Are you okay?"

Ilia shook herself from her thoughts. She nodded.

"Surely you've seen a Water Mage before." He grinned at her, his face colouring.

Ilia smiled and stared at the ground ahead of her. "Well, yes, but in the potions labs, not the training grounds."

Eri shrugged. "I'm passable with potions. I can make a salve to heal the bumps and scrapes from training, but I prefer to buy the potions. If Master needs more healing than I can manage, I want to be ready. Mostly I use them on myself. He's too good with a sword, and I'm still gaining experience."

The big knight chuckled. "He's doing well. Best student in the Guard right now."

"Only student in the Guard," Eri loudly whispered behind his hand at her.

Ilia giggled and slapped a hand over her mouth.

She walked quietly with them for a while, possibly hours with how her legs felt, sharing easy banter and listening to stories of Eri's early training. She shared her experiences training with the Champion, and Eri listened to every detail. Ilia taught Eri some quick healing spells for minor injuries as they walked. The soft soil cushioned her feet well and was comfortable to walk on. She loved feeling the dirt between her toes.

"We'll have a snack before we keep going." The big knight glanced around. "This is as good a spot as any."

"Rations, Master?"

"We can forage easily, too." Ilia pointed at the herbs growing beneath some trees, protected by their roots.

"Those are edible?" Eri narrowed his eyes at the little flowering plants.

Ilia kneeled beside the plants. "Nutritious, too. Look for some with at least three flowers open. Pinch them off just above the lowest leaves like this. The whole top part can be eaten, leaves and all. Try one." She pinched the plant off and handed it to Eri. Ilia harvested another for herself, and one for the big knight. She took a bite and chewed slowly, tasting the sweetness of the flowers on her tongue.

"Hey, this is pretty good," Eri mumbled around his mouthful.

Ilia swallowed. "At this time of year, there are all kinds of plants we can eat, right here around us." Ilia closed her eyes and felt around in the soil. She took a few steps and kneeled. With a touch of Earth Magic, Ilia exposed some roots. "These are best cooked over a fire with some berries, but they're edible raw, too." She pinched a few off and pulled them from the soil. Ilia handed some roots to each man.

"Master Silvan taught you all this?" The big knight took the roots and chewed some.

Ilia nodded. "I harvest herbs for her private collection all the time, so she taught me which plants to eat, which had to be cooked first, and which are useful for potions or medicine. If I'm gathering all day, I don't need to carry food. The forest provides."

"Okay, I can see the flowering plants, but you just knew the roots were there. How?" Eri crouched beside her, his elbows on his knees as he looked down at the roots.

She laughed. "Plant Mage, remember? I've been doing this since I was small."

The big knight swallowed the last of his roots. "How are you to keep walking?" He held her gaze with his piercing green eyes.

"I'll be okay." Hopefully.

He nodded. "Let's go."

***

"The city isn't far now, but we'll spend the night here." The big knight slipped his pack from his shoulders and let it slide to the ground.

Ilia dropped to the grass and closed her eyes. Thank the Spirits. Could she take another step if she needed to?

"You're sure, Master?" Eri glanced through the trees towards lights in the distance.

"You want to carry her?" The big knight folded his arms over his chest.

"The tent, Master?"

Ilia rolled and looked up at them.

"Full camp. We'll leave in the morning, when we're all rested. I'll prepare the meal." He rustled in his pack and pulled out a bag.

"Yes, Master." Eri took his pack off and pulled a larger bag from inside.

Ilia pushed herself up to sit. Should she help? She didn't know how to camp. It wasn't her fault her only night experience in the forest was sneaking out for walks, or the occasional special herb collection mission. No, this was her chance to learn.

Ilia forced herself to her feet and joined Eri. "Can I help?"

"Sure. Set this out where we want it and tap it."

"Tap it?"

"Like this." Eri shook the tent out and set the corner on the ground. He tapped the cloth twice.

Ilia backed up as the tent unfolded and rose. The poles unfolded and slid themselves into place, supporting the tent now. At a snap of his fingers, the bedrolls flew from his pack and zipped into the tent. A blanket flew past her face, rustling her hair in the breeze.

"That's incredible," she whispered. Ilia stared at the tent. "What does it look like inside?"

"Take a look." Eri pulled the tent flap back and gestured for her to go in.

Ilia stepped through the opening. A mage-light lamp hung on the center pole, glowing brightly. Filtered daylight streamed through the fabric. Two bedrolls were unrolled and ready on one side of the tent. A blanket lay spread out on the other side.

"Our packs and such go over there, too." Eri pointed towards the blanket. "You can sleep there tonight. We don't have a spare bedroll, but the blanket should be warm enough. If it's not, let us know."

"I'll be fine." Ilia sniffed the air. She knew those herbs.

"Smells good, huh?" Eri smiled.

"It does. Brings back fond memories of the castle kitchens. Healer training."

"What? Healer training included cooking?"

Ilia shrugged. "You can fix a lot for a person by paying attention to their diet. Proper nutrition helps us stay healthy. Besides, most herbs have medicinal properties, too. When food tastes better, people are more likely to take their herbal medicine in it."

"If you two are done doing—whatever you're doing—there's more to do out here."

"Coming, Master." Eri grinned. He nodded to the tent opening.

Ilia stepped from the tent, brushing the flap aside. The massive knight sat at the campfire, stirring a pot. She smiled at the fresh herbs and cooking vegetables. Stew. Her stomach growled. She walked closer and saw the brightly coloured vegetables in the thick broth.

Eri waved at his pack and bowls and spoons skidded out, flying over to the big man and resting beside him. He snapped his fingers and mumbled. Small thick rugs zipped over, settling around the fire. Ilia glanced down and noticed the big knight already sitting on one. Eri lowered himself to a little carpet and nodded at the last one.

"Wash first, then we eat." The big knight gestured to a pot of water sitting near the fire.

Eri summoned a couple of metal bowls from his pack and moved to the pot. He dipped them in the pot and handed one to Ilia, along with a cloth. Eri settled back on his rug and began washing. Ilia lowered herself to the last rug. The fibers were soft under her and protected her from the cooler ground.

"Dirt begone, hygiene strong," Ilia mumbled, and snapped her fingers.

The dirt and dust fell from her and Eri and landed back in the surrounding soil. Ilia dipped her cloth in the water and washed her face and hands. She scrubbed her feet. The dirt might be gone, but she'd been walking all day without shoes. Ilia sighed as she massaged her feet.

"Good. Here. Eat up. We get an early night after that."

She took the steaming bowl of stew from the big knight and cradled it in her hands. Thank goodness for the magic protecting me from the heat, she thought, as she held the warm bowl.

Eri snapped his fingers, and their wash water flew to the nearest tree, settling into the soil around the roots. Ilia watched as she tucked into her stew, gulping it down after cooling each spoonful with a little Air Magic.

When her bowl was empty, she set it on the ground near her little carpet. Ilia watched the fire, the flames dancing around the logs, lulling her with their hypnotic movements. Her eyes dropped closed.

***

Ilia blinked and rubbed her eyes. She'd fallen asleep beside the fire and woke wrapped in her blankets in the tent. They got up early, ate and packed, and left the forest as the sun rose over the trees. The city was ahead, clearly visible now, with the forest behind them. "Aren't there spells for dust control on these roads?" she mumbled.

Eri took her hand and pulled her to the side of the road. A large wagon rumbled past, packed full of barrels and crates. More dust rose around her, and Ilia coughed.

"You act like you've never been on a busy road before." Eri smiled.

Ilia stared down at her feet. Her cheeks burned. "I haven't."

Eri raised his eyebrow.

"Master Silvan took me in as a baby. I haven't been far from the castle, except to forage for herbs, or by carriage when she took me to heal some nobles. I've never been this far from home."

Eri took her hand and gave it a light squeeze. "Mithlan's not as big as Dinlark. It doesn't have a wall or anything, but it's a massive trading city. We need to watch for wagons, and some don't make near enough noise."

Ilia bumped into him as she shifted away from a small wagon speeding past. She waved back at the smiling driver as he headed towards the forest, fresh from the city and any trading he did. "What do they trade?" She stared at the goods bundled in sacks, piled high in the small wagon.

"Anything. Everything. If it's legal to trade, it's here." The big knight pulled her aside as another wagon sped past, this one going to the city. "There's an underground market here as well, but we're getting it shut down."

Eri quickened his pace, pulling her with him. Ilia hustled to keep up, her feet slapping the packed dirt. Another wagon rolled past, coming from the city. The driver wore colourful embroidered robes, easily visible, perched up in the control seat.

"We stay on this side of the road while on foot, so wagons are coming at us. We can see them from farther away this way. You don't want to be run over from behind, and there's less risk of stepping out in front of one by mistake." Eri slowed his step for her.

Ilia moved closer to Eri, closer to the road's edge. She tilted her head and listened. The familiar forest sounds were gone, replaced by distant voices calling ahead, mumbles she'd never pick from the mess of sound.

CHAPTER 7

THE BIG CITY

The crops and fields on either side of the road were quiet. The occasional worker moved among the plants, tending the orchards or checking the fields of young grain crops. A few spring vegetables were being harvested in distant fields.

"Most of the country's food is grown here." The big knight guided her from a wagon's path with a large hand on her shoulder. "It's partly why Mithlan is the primary trading hub."

There was so much to see, all the crops and fields, drivers in brightly coloured clothing, wagons of all shapes and sizes, and even a farm with horses near the road. Eri moved her to his other side, closer to the road edge.

Wagons came regularly now, from the small private wagons to the massive cargo loads. Some carried fresh vegetables to the city, others carried covered loads away. The noises grew louder, reminding her of the mass of people at the royal balls or public court sessions.

Ilia looked down. The packed dirt gave way to cobblestones. Wagon wheels clattered on the new surface, adding to the noise. How did people stand it, all the yelling and banging and clattering? Was it bad form to cover her ears?

They passed into the city, walking down wide streets with stone buildings on either side. People stayed at the edges while wagons navigated the middle of the streets. Eri tucked her along beside the buildings as the big knight moved ahead to lead them through the congested traffic.

He turned down another wide street. Eri guided Ilia along, around vendors set up at the side of the road, merchants in luxurious clothing calling to the crowds. Her hand tightened on Eri's as she noticed people in little more than rags sitting in shady alleys or tucked in behind the merchants, out of the sun.

She sighed and relaxed her tight muscles as they turned down a quieter side street. Ilia clung to his hand. If she got separated now, she'd never find them again. The noises seemed just a little quieter down this way, away from the worst of the crowds and wagons.

The massive knight stopped at a thick wooden door. He opened it and stepped inside. Eri guided her in. The door closed with a thud and the metal latch clicked in place. Ilia moved closer to Eri and clung to his hand.

Ilia glanced around swiftly as the massive knight marched to the stairs along a side wall. A man sat at a desk near the door, quill on parchment and head down as he wrote. Two women played cards at a small table nearby, both dressed in tunics and trousers like the big knight. She noticed a sword on one woman's belt before they hustled her up the stairs.

She climbed each step as quickly as she could, trying to keep up. They passed a second floor and kept going, stopping on the third and top floor. Ilia gasped for breath as he opened the door and disappeared through it.

"Ready?" Eri smiled.

Ilia took a slow breath and nodded.

Eri opened the door and stepped aside. "Go on in."

Ilia smiled and looked around, strolling across the room. The walls had massive open arches in them, giving her a good view of most of the city. She looked back out over the crops and to the forest beyond them. They were close to the edge of the city.

She glanced around for the big knight. The breeze rustled her hair. She adjusted her headscarf, knowing it was pointless. Her wild, light brown hair did what it pleased. Ilia darted past mirrors hanging on the stone pillars and supports, bowls of water on pedestals, and crystal balls on metal stands.

"Over here." The big knight stood near the far wall, next to a gigantic mirror with a wide gold frame.

Ilia sped over to his side.

A woman appeared beside them. Ilia jumped back, bumping into Eri. He steadied her with his hands on her shoulders.

"Who would you like to contact, Ser?" She raised her hand towards the mirror.

"Master Silvan, with the Castle Healers."

"Right away, Ser." Her dark robes flowed as she moved. The woman touched the mirror, and the surface filled with fog.

The fog flowed, shifted, and swirled, spiraling in towards the middle of the mirror. Ilia held her stomach and closed her eyes. Please, breakfast, stay put.

Eri chuckled. His hands on her shoulders squeezed lightly. "Don't look," he whispered, his mouth near her ear. "It does that to most people." Eri wrapped an arm around her and let her lean back against him.

Ilia felt steadier, her small body leaning against Eri's solid muscle. No, don't think that. Her cheeks burned.

"Brannon, thank the Spirits. Is she okay?"

Ilia's eyes popped open at the familiar sound. Her heart ached at the frantic sound of Master Silvan's voice.

The big knight bowed. "She's fine. We took the trip a little slower for her, and she handled it with no problems." He turned and took Ilia's hand, guiding her in front of the mirror.

"Ilia, what were you thinking? I wake to a note fluttering in front of my face that you're in the forest. I didn't know what to think. If you hadn't been found by the Knight-Master, anything could have happened to you. What were you doing outside? Do you still have the crystal?" Master Silvan narrowed her eyes at the girl.

Ilia pulled the chain up and showed her the crystal, still glowing in the fine metal netting at the end. "I had a nightmare. I think it was just a nightmare. I needed fresh air."

"That explains how you ended up outside despite my instructions not to leave. It doesn't explain how you ended up so far from the castle. When you get back, you're restricted to the Healing Wing and Garden, young lady. Brannon, how quickly can you send her back?"

"I'll have to check. I don't know when the next official wagon leaves, or if any knights are heading back and can escort her. We'll keep her safe until then." The big knight bowed his head.

"See that you do. She needs to get back as soon as possible. Oh, get her some shoes and robes for travel. I'll pay you back when you return."

He smiled at Master Silvan. "I know you will. She'll be back as soon as I can arrange it."

The mirror grew cloudy, and Master Silvan disappeared. The woman was at a crystal ball, staring into its reflections, and she wandered over. When she touched the mirror frame, it returned to a reflective surface.

Knight-Master Brannon gazed down at Ilia. "Do you need a rest before we get you some boots? Are you hungry?"

Ilia squirmed. "I'm fine." Would she be, going back into that mass of people and the noise they made?

"Come, then." The big knight strode from the room.

Ilia watched him go. Eri nudged her and smiled. She smiled back before scurrying after the big man. She caught up at the door and slipped through behind him. He descended the stairs, stopping at the second floor.

She followed him into a hallway with doors on both sides. Mage-light lamps gave a warm yellowish glow, and daylight streamed in through the window at the end. He walked nearly to the window before stopping at a solid wood door. He opened it and stepped aside, waving for her to go in.

Ilia took a few steps inside and stopped. Eri squeezed past her, walked to one of two sturdy wooden-framed beds, and set his pack down beside it. The Knight-Master guided her in a few more steps with a hand on her back. He walked to the other bed and dropped his pack on the floor.

She took a moment to really look around as the big knight rustled in his pack. There was a table with maps spread over it, and a couple of chairs neatly tucked in. A bookshelf sat against another wall, though she couldn't read the titles from here.

"We're going to the market. It'll be busy and you'll see people from all over the country there, maybe even some non-magical folk from across the border. Stay close, and don't wander if we get separated." The big knight straightened up, a coin pouch in his hand.

"Yes, Knight-Master," she whispered.

Eri set a hand on her shoulder. "I'll make sure she's okay."

The big knight nodded. "Let's go."

She followed him from the room, with Eri behind her again. Ilia smiled. It was comforting, having someone who cared what happened to her. Master Silvan was like that, despite her brisk manner with others.

Ilia glanced back up at Eri as they walked down the hallway. "Do you come to the city often? Aren't you stationed at the castle?"

"We are, but we regularly travel to the big cities. The Castle Guard works closely with the regular knights, and we're even chosen from within those ranks." Eri's steps were quieter than she expected on the wooden floor.

"Oh." That made sense, really. Knight-Master Brannon ran the Castle Guards, but that didn't mean he guarded the King personally. He probably had a lot of things to keep track of and do to keep the castle safe.

The city noises hit Ilia as she stepped from the building behind the big knight. The inside must be shielded, like the infirmary, so people could rest and plan and such in peace. She gripped the doorframe and steadied herself. Eri rested a warm hand against her back, giving her a moment to catch her breath.

"Thank you," she whispered. Ilia straightened up and squared her shoulders.

The big knight glanced back and waited a few paces away. Ilia scurried after him, Eri matching her pace easily with his long stride. They headed back to the main road and joined the throng of people passing deeper into the city.

Eri took her hand and stepped beside her. Ilia gripped his hand. People didn't seem to understand personal space, and the crowd jostled her, knocking her about. Eri pulled her closer and draped an arm over her shoulders. He eased her to the edge of the street. Ilia could breathe again.

Her head spun to the right. A massive window showed a store packed with books, shelves everywhere inside. She stared at it as long as she could, before the crowd hid it from view. How many books were in there? She bumped against Eri as she took a long last glance back.

They passed under a large archway covered in bright paint. Knight-Master Brannon led them through the marketplace. Tents and stalls stood in rows and rows that seemed to go on forever. Bright fabric canopies protected merchants and their goods from the sun.

He led them along a side path with booths of leatherworkers fixing items or calling to the crowds, showing off their products. She'd never seen so many styles and colours of boots in her life. Hats and handbags hung from hooks and poles, some brightly dyed and ornate, others more utilitarian.

The big knight stopped at a smaller corner booth. Sturdy boots lined the table and shelves, with belt pouches and knife sheaths on another rack. Leather messenger bags and packs lined part of the back wall. Everything was black or brown, shining brightly and newly polished.

"Knight-Master Brannon. Always a pleasure." A cheerful older woman with greying hair stood from her chair in a corner. A pair of partly finished boots sat on a little table beside her. "What can I get you today?"

The big man smiled. "She needs some boots, sturdy and good for cross-country travel and the forest."

Ilia smiled shyly. "Hi."

"Hello, girl. Come around here and sit, and I'll get you taken care of." The woman pulled the tent flap back and Ilia darted around the table. "Can you clean your feet yourself?"

"Yes, Ma'am." Ilia settled into the chair. She waved her hand over her feet and the dirt fell, gathered into a little pile, and scooted out under the back of the tent.

"Clever child. Most young people let the dirt fall on my carpet."

Ilia looked down at the brightly coloured carpet, a beautiful and stylized forest landscape with a mountain in the background. "It's a lovely rug."

"I like this girl." The woman beamed up at the big knight. She turned and scanned a shelf of smaller boots on the side wall, selecting a pair of brown boots that would go up over Ilia's ankles. "Try these."

Ilia pulled the boots onto her clean feet. The leather was soft inside, and the boots conformed to her feet like a second skin. If she stepped wrong, the outside was strong enough to protect her ankles from rolling.

The woman kneeled in front of her and checked the fit, her fingers pressing in firmly. "I thought they'd work well. Do you like the colour?"

Ilia smiled. "Brown is fine. It reminds me of the tree trunks."

The woman laughed. "A girl after my own heart." She stood and turned to the men. "Do you want it on your account?"

"Here." The big knight handed her a small pouch that jingled with the sound of coins.

She reached over the table and took the pouch. "Would you prefer change, or are you looking for something else as well?"

"I could use a new knife sheath." The big man nodded.

"Master, may I take Ilia to the bookseller's store?"

The big man stared at Eri for a few slow heartbeats. "Go ahead. Take her straight back when you're done. I need to arrange her ride back, and some travel robes."

Ilia grinned at Eri. He held his hand out and she darted from the stall. She slid her hand into his.

"Thank you." Ilia waved at the woman as Eri led her away.

"You're welcome, child. Enjoy the books."

She glanced back as Eri led her through the crowd. The knight had a polished utility belt in his hands. The crowd closed around her. She gripped Eri's hand tighter and moved closer to him. Just how many people lived here?

How could they stand this? She took a deep breath and let it out slowly as Eri moved to the edge of the crowd and out of the market.

CHAPTER 8

DRAGONS AND BOOKSTORES

E ri opened the door and led Ilia inside the store. She wandered in, her gaze darting about at all the books. Every inch of the walls were covered in shelves. The middle was all shelves back-to-back, filled with books and scrolls.

"Not quite the castle library, huh?" Eri walked through the store towards a set of shelves in the far corner.

"It's wonderful." She followed him slowly, glancing at book titles along the way.

A book caught her eye, shining gold lettering against a worn dark leather cover. She stopped and slid it from the shelf. Ilia flipped through the pages slowly, looking at the bright illustrations of dragons.

"This isn't a library. If you want to read the whole thing, buy it."

Ilia glanced at the man behind the counter. He scowled at her. Ilia frowned. Her money was back at the castle. She so seldom needed it, she never carried any with her.

"What did you find?" Eri appeared beside her, with an armload of books.

"Dragons: A Guide, by E.J. Warder." She closed the book and let him see the cover.

"Wow. He was that big naturalist a century ago. You want it?" Eri grinned at her.

Ilia blinked up at him. Was he really offering? "Oh, yes, please," she whispered.

Eri held his hand out and she gave him the book. It was hard letting go of all that precious information, but it was about to be hers. He took the stack of books to the counter. Ilia watched the books as the seller noted them on the little receipt. Swordsmanship and Spells, Intermediate Battle Tactics, and Help, My Sword Won't Light.

He counted out the coins while she fidgeted beside him. What would she learn from that book? Could it help her?

"It was a pleasure doing business with you." The man smiled, though his scowl lines were deep. "Please, come again."

Eri tucked the books under his arm and took Ilia's hand. Ilia opened the door, and they headed out into the street. She forgot all about the crowds and her discomfort. She had a new book. He led her all the way back to the room on the second floor, her mind on her book the entire way.

"Here." He set his books on the table and handed her the thick leather-bound book. "You can relax on my bed and read if you like. You might be more comfortable."

Ilia bounded over and settled on the soft mattress. She propped herself up on the pillow and leaned back against the headboard. Her fingers brushed over the textured leather, still in good shape, though worn from decades of use. She opened the book and started reading.

Dragons mate for life. Interesting. If one dies, the other will seek a new mate, but not without exacting revenge on the murderer. Prepare for retribution. She stared blankly at the wall across from her. There haven't been any dragon attacks reported, no flaming cities or mass damage. Is the retribution limited to the attacker?

Ilia glanced at Eri. He had a book propped open on the table and had a short wooden practice sword in his hands. He raised his arms overhead and sliced diagonally down, his face set in concentration. She dropped her gaze to the page again. The paper was thin and worn, but still strong.

Dragons don't eat people or livestock. In fact, nobody has ever seen a dragon eat at all. Nests are clean, no sign of excrement. They seem to survive on the magic in the land, transforming it and exuding new magic through their skin and scales. Mages have reported magic being more potent when near a dragon. They'd observed a fog rising from sleeping dragons when the lighting has been right, so this theory needs more testing.

Ilia narrowed her eyes at the page. Dragons eat magic? How's that possible? Magic exists in everything, the land and forests, and the people in her country, and even some animals like wolves were full of it. What happens if the dragons disappear? Is the librarian right, and they change magic into a useable form somehow? Could we still use magic without the dragons, or will it be locked away, out of our reach forever? Ilia rubbed her temples.

"Are you okay?" Eri paused, his practice sword outstretched in a thrust.

"I'm fine." Ilia smiled. "There's a lot of information here, and I'm trying to take it all in."

The door swung open, and Knight-Master Brannon strode into the room. He set some parchment pages on the table beside Eri's book. "Raise that elbow."

Eri adjusted his position, lifting his elbow, and his sword changed angle slightly.

"Good. Now the blade will slide between their armour better, and you have an open channel in your arms for your energy to pass into the blade." Brannon turned to Ilia. "There are a couple of knights returning to the castle on a small transport wagon late this afternoon. You'll go with them. Here, I got you new robes. Change in there are leave my tunic folded on the shelf."

Ilia pressed her lips together. She nodded. Could she safely go back? What about the black knight? She slipped from the bed and took the robes from him. The dark green fabric was soft in her hands, a fine cotton and wool blend with a lined linen cloak. This would keep her warm through a wagon ride at night.

She stepped into the bathroom and closed the door. The bathroom was small, but still felt spacious. There was a sink and toilet, and a bathtub big enough for the large knight. Ilia smiled at the fluffy towels. How good would it feel to wrap up in those after a luxurious hot bath?

In moments, she changed clothes. Ilia folded the tunic and set it on the shelf for him. The cloth shifted and adjusted on her body, snugging up in a few places to fit her perfectly. Ilia glanced at herself in the long mirror by the bathtub and nodded. Green always looked good on her.

Ilia returned to Eri's bed and picked up her book. Her eyes scanned the page, but her brain didn't want to register the words she read. No, she needed to find out whether it was just a dream. Was there someone here who could help her? Dinlark had the advanced magic school. Was there even a magic school here in Mithlan?

"Can I get myself a snack?" Ilia closed her book and set it down.

The big knight looked up from his papers on the table. He frowned.

Oh, please, she pleaded in her head. Let me go, please.

The big knight nodded. "Eri?"

"I'll show you where the kitchen is." Eri set his practice sword down and headed for the door. "Come with me."

"Bring a tea back, would you?"

Eri smiled. "Yes, Master."

Ilia glanced at her book. There was so much in the book she hadn't seen yet, so much to learn, but she couldn't take it with her. This might be her only chance to get away. Ilia slipped from the bed and followed Eri from the room.

"Do you stay here often?" It was hard not to whisper in these narrow stone halls.

Eri nodded. "Often enough for us to have permanent rooms here. We come each month, roughly, depending on what rumors we're tracking down, or what operations we're on." He led her down the stairs and to the main floor. Eri nodded at the women, still playing cards at the little table.

Horse dirt, Ilia cursed to herself. How was she going to sneak past them? There better be another way out. Ilia followed him down a windowless hall past the women, with many doors on either side.

"What are all these rooms? More bedrooms?" Ilia brushed her fingers over a door as she passed.

Eri opened a door and stepped back. "Storage, see?"

The room was full of boxes and crates. Two large windows looked out into the alley, their shutters open to let light and air inside.

Eri followed her gaze and smiled. "Yeah, those have security on them. We can leave them open any time, but nobody can come in from outside. We've never had a theft here, even with so many people around."

"Neat." Is it a one-way spell? Can she leave through them?

"How about that snack?" Eri closed the door. He took two steps and crossed the hall, opening another door for her.

Warm baking smells rushed over her as Eri opened this door. Ilia stepped inside and felt the heat from the ovens. Pots of stew bubbled on stoves and over fires, and another meal cooked in a pan where a woman stood beside it, stirring. Other people moved around, tending the fires and watching the meals.

"There are fruit and rolls in the bowls here," Eri gestured at a long table. "Help yourself. I'll get the tea." He walked across the room to a stove with kettles, near a table with teapots and mugs.

Ilia selected an apple and pear from a basket. Eri poured water into a teapot, his back to her. She slipped out the door and across the hall. Ilia grasped the cold metal handle and turned it, the latch releasing with a click. She eased through the small gap and let the door close behind her.

She stuffed the fruit in her pockets and dashed to the windows, weaving around the crates. At the window, she stopped. Ilia reached her hand out through the opening. Nothing felt odd, nothing prevented her from pulling her hand back. Ilia boosted herself up and wriggled through the large opening. She landed lightly in the alley.

A quick glance around proved she was alone, except for a man in tattered clothing sitting in the shade of a large crate. "Spare a coin, Miss?" His weathered face disguised his age, but his greying hair and thin frame showed he wasn't young anymore.

"I don't have any coins, but you can have this." Ilia pulled the apple from her pocket and held it out to him.

"Bless you, Miss."

Ilia held a finger to her lips, and he nodded. She darted down the alley and stopped at the street. People wandered past, filling the edges of the street as wagons rumbled down the middle. Ilia pulled her cloak hood up. If she could make it across the street without being squished by a cart, she might make it past to the gate unseen. Were they even looking yet?

Ilia took a deep breath and let it out. After the next wagon, she darted into the traffic and dodged a small speeding cart.

Could she find her way back out? She longed for the forest, for the familiar safety of the trees.

She tucked behind a massive wagon, rumbling along at a brisk walking pace. Ilia moved around it until she couldn't see the building over the massive pile of goods under the wagon's tarp. This just might work. The wagon turned at the main crossroads, and Ilia followed it all the way through the main gates onto the dirt road.

Her boots were comfortable and supported her feet well. She barely felt when the cobblestones turned to packed dirt underfoot. The wagon picked up speed. Ilia jogged to keep up. Her empty stomach growled in protest. She was going to miss lunch, but the forest had more than enough if she made it that far.

"You okay, Miss?" The wagon slowed, and a woman leaned over the side.

Ilia nodded. "I'm just going home." Well, not really, but would she believe the truth? She didn't want to get sent back to the city.

"Where are you headed?" Sharp blue eyes fixed on her. The woman raised an eyebrow.

Ilia pointed south. Please, let there be a settlement or something out that way. Her education had mostly been about herbalism and healing. How could her knowledge of geography be so lacking?

The wagon stopped, and the woman eased herself from the control seat. She landed lightly beside Ilia, despite being older. "What brings you to Mithlan? You're not running away, are you? Who's your master?"

Ilia stood quietly, her gaze down on her new boots, a fine layer of dust covering the shiny leather.

The woman peered in at her neckband. "Master Silvan? Really? Aren't you going the wrong way?"

CHAPTER 9

ON THE ROAD

I lia shook her head. "I was in the forest checking the herbs. She likes to know how healthy the plants are. I'd never been in the city before, so I thought I'd stop by. I just have a few more places to check before I go back."

"Hop on. I'll give you a ride to the tree line. She really lets you wander the forest by yourself, so far from the castle?"

Ilia nodded. Don't fidget, she reminded herself. "She taught me what I needed to know, and I can collect any herb for her at all, no matter how rare. I've been doing this for years." Even if I've never camped before, she added to herself. The odd night under the stars with no tent didn't count, not to her.

The woman reached up and grabbed a shiny handle. She pulled herself up the small steps and back onto the smooth wooden bench. At her nod, Ilia reached up and gripped the handle. She stretched to reach each toe hold, her boots gripping the rubber easily.

She settled on the bench and peered over the side. Her fingers turned white as she saw how far down it was.

"First wagon ride?" The woman gave Ilia's knee a warm squeeze.

Ilia nodded. "On such a large and beautiful wagon like this, yes. I've only been in carriages."

The woman grinned. "She's a beauty, isn't she? Better to be up here, above the dust, and in the fresh air. This wagon can take the biggest loads possible."

The wagon rolled, slow and ponderous, but it picked up speed smoothly. The packed dirt road was smoothed as well, and Ilia barely felt the motion, but for the breeze on her face. She clutched the seat edge and wagon side. There was nothing in front of her to keep her from falling off and being run over, no front wall of any kind, just an angled footrest to brace against.

Her stomach growled again, reminding her of her missed snack. Ilia pulled her pear from her pocket. "May I snack?"

The woman smiled. "Go ahead. Clean up any sticky juices, mind."

"I will."

Ilia bit into the pear. Sweet pear juice flowed into her mouth. She slurped it up as quietly as she could, but some fruits were just noisier to eat than others. Once in the forest, she could forage, but this would work for now. No, don't glance back at the city. They might watch her from the communication tower, she reminded herself.

The wagon sped towards the forest, smooth and fast. While not as speedy as the smaller wagon she saw earlier, Ilia still blinked in the breeze, her eyes threatening to water. She sighed when the wagon rolled into the trees and the shade blanketed the area from the leafy canopy. Ilia tossed her pear in the trees and snapped her fingers. A few drops of pear juice flew into the bushes.

The woman guided the wagon to the edge of the road, and it rolled to a gentle stop. "Are you sure I can't take you farther?"

"Thank you so much for the ride. I really am grateful, but I have a few things to do before I go back. I'll be home in no time." Ilia swallowed hard. Sure, she was used to keeping calm for the sickest patients, but this was challenging her abilities to stretch the truth. She lowered herself from the wagon and stepped back.

"Take care of yourself, now. There have been strange tales of men in black armour going through the taverns. Each tale is wilder than the last. Even if it's just bandits, a girl travelling alone has cause for worry." The woman waved at her.

Ilia waved back. "I will. I know the forests, and I'll be fine." She smiled widely.

The wagon rolled away, and Ilia left the road. She wandered idly as her mind ran over everything she knew. Should she go back after all? Would everyone be in danger if she did? It was probably a dream, wasn't it? It didn't feel like a dream. Was the man in the dream even looking for her, or was she just there?

Ilia scowled. Dreams were the absolute worst form of divination. You forget so much. Things are hazy in the dream state, and the mind can be so suggestible. She needed another method. Master Silvan wasn't here, so maybe it was time to try the new techniques she read about.

Okay, I'll need a bowl and some water, right from the stream is best.

She walked slowly over the soft soil and cushioning mosses, deeper into the trees. Ilia let her senses blanket the forest around her, feeling for what she needed. Bowls can be clay or wood, but there's no clay here.

After a few minutes of walking, Ilia found a tree the right size that fell, leaving a big stump with a jagged surface. She rubbed her hands together and gathered her Earth Magic. Once her hands were warm and her palms tingled, she plucked wood from the stump and formed it into a ball in her hands like a potter works with clay.

Ilia kneaded the wooden fibers together and shaped them into a bowl. No, it needs to be more even than that. She worked the wood steadily until her bowl was as symmetrical as she could get it. There, that should do it. Now, for a source of water.

She listened and opened herself to the forest, to the surrounding plants. She listened with her normal senses. Forest, can you help me, she pleaded.

A breeze blew through, picking up leaves and swirling them around. They scattered to the southeast, blowing between the trees. Ilia smiled. She held her bowl carefully in one hand and followed the leaves. Within minutes, she heard the bubbling of a fast-flowing stream. Ilia dashed ahead, following the sound. The leaves dropped, and the breeze returned to normal.

Thank you, forest.

Shimmering light reflected through the trees ahead, sunlight dancing on the water's surface. Ilia darted over. A shallow stream flowed from the south, clear rushing water. Perfect. She kneeled and scooped up the water, the cold numbing her fingers quickly.

Ilia moved back and settled beneath a tree, her back to the rough wood. She peered down into the bowl at her distorted reflection. No, sit still and let it settle. She looked again. Her face looked back at her, but her skin was a rich brown and her hair was green and looked like moss. Ilia blinked. The image winked at her and faded.

What did she just see? Was she going forest crazy? It could happen to herbalists who spent too much time alone. She shook her head and closed her eyes. Ilia meditated with slow and deep breaths, her bowl on the grass in front of her, as she waited for the water to settle.

I can do this. Calmly now, and slow breaths. Mind like a mirror.

She peered into the bowl, leaning over the water, her hands on either side of the bowl to support herself. Where are the dragons? The water rippled. Hazy shapes appeared on the water's surface. The shapes swirled and reformed, some areas growing darker, and others got lighter.

Not clear enough. Ilia closed her eyes and waited, taking more slow breaths. She opened her eyes again. The shapes coloured, the upper part turning blue. The jagged lower part was a dull grey. Mountains? Were the dragons in the mountains?

Probably, actually. Dragons were seldom seen now, and the mountains were mostly uninhabited, except for a few hardy souls. Okay, which mountains, though? Southeast or west? She narrowed her eyes and scanned the image. Even the smallest detail might help.

"Ilia!"

She jumped, her heart racing. Her hand knocked against the bowl, sending the water flying. Some splashed over her hand. Pain raced through her body. Ilia gasped and collapsed, her arm giving out. Her elbow ached and her right thigh burned, like someone was stabbing her with a hot poker. Ilia closed her eyes and pressed her hands to her temples, her head pounding with her pulse.

"Ilia, what's wrong?" Knight-Master Brannon kneeled beside her, his enormous hands supporting her as he cradled her head and sat her up.

Tears streamed down her face. She panted for air. The pain crushed down on her, making her ribs ache.

"Breathe easy, now, healer." He leaned her forward over one arm and Ilia could breathe a little easier. The big knight rubbed her back slowly, warmth flowing from his hand into her. "Are you okay? I feel the pain but can't find any wounds."

Ilia wiped her tears with her soft sleeve. "I'm unhurt. I think another dragon has been injured, though."

He helped her sit upright and let her lean against him. "Did it happen again?"

"Did what happen again?" Eri kneeled on her other side.

"She felt the last dragon as it died."

Eri blinked. "Are you kidding me? How?"

Ilia shrugged. Her body trembled and she couldn't stop it. "I don't know. I thought I was going to die last time. This time it just hurt really badly."

The big knight held her as Eri wrapped a blanket around her. "Can you feel where it is? Can we help in any way?"

"It's in the mountains. That's all I learned before—" She stared down at the bowl nearby, misshapen from where she bumped it.

"Before we interrupted you." The big knight rubbed her back again, his arm still around her.

Ilia nodded.

Eri picked up the bowl. "You were scrying in this?" He turned the bowl over in his hands. "You made this here moments ago, didn't you?"

"I didn't think it would work," she whispered.

"Take a sip of this." The big knight reached into his pack and pulled out a canteen. He uncapped it and dropped two herbal tablets inside. He brought it up to her lips and supported the canteen for her.

Ilia sipped the water. The herbs were bitter, but energy rushed through her body and her shaking stopped. Her breathing eased to normal again. No more ache at all. Ilia smiled to herself. Those were fresh. They might even be the tablets she helped Master Silvan make the other day.

She took a few more long sips. "Thank you. How did you find me?"

"Master Silvan has given me temporary guardianship over you. I called her when we realized you were missing. Now I can feel roughly where you are, so we followed. Why did you leave?" He stared down at her, holding her in place with his sharp gaze.

"I can't go back," she whispered, her voice cracking. "I had a vision, or dream, or something like that. They all died. The black knight killed them. I think he wanted me, and they died because they were between me and him."

Eri raised an eyebrow. "You ran because of a dream?"

The big knight shook his head. "If she can scry, her dream might be a warning. If the castle is in danger, we need to act. We need to go back, and now. If there's danger, that's where we should be." He tucked the canteen away.

"I have to help the dragon. I heard Master Dinoc and Master Silvan arguing. He thinks magic might stop working if the dragons die. Do you want to lose your magic?" She turned pleading eyes on the big knight.

He frowned. "He said that?"

Ilia nodded. "He seemed so sure. I've never heard him argue with anyone like that. He said if we save the dragons, we save all of us." Well, he said 'might,' I think, but I won't tell them that.

"Master, Champion Loni is still at the castle. Send her a message. She can work with Knight-Master Holden to guard everyone." Eri held out a quill and parchment.

Knight-Master Brannon stared at the parchment. Ilia sat quietly. The same thing that urged her to run was probably telling him to go back. I need to find the dragons, though. Let me go, please.

"Mountains, huh?" Eri smiled at her. "Do you know which ones?"

Ilia glanced up at the peaks visible through the break in the trees from the stream. "Those look right." Maybe.

The big knight glanced up. "We're hours away at best."

Eri scowled. "Will we make it? How badly injured is the dragon?"

"We have one chance, a distant hope, and it might not work." Knight-Master Brannon raised his hand and muttered. "We can follow the magical currents. We'll be turned into spirits and can ride the currents as close as we can get. When we arrive, we'll turn physical again. It's dangerous, and there's a chance we can get lost or be split up."

The air shimmered. Massive strands of magic and power glowed in the air above the forest.

"There's one we can use." The big knight pointed to where the glowing strand came close to them. He looked down at Ilia.

She squirmed under his gaze but held his eye contact. Did she really want to be turned into energy and whisked away somewhere, maybe to not turn back? How mad would Master Silvan be? What happened if she rematerialized, but something trapped them, leaving her with an injured dragon and whoever was trying to kill it?

CHAPTER 10

Taking a Chance

"It's worth the risk, though, right?" Eri walked towards the glowing current, where it dipped from the sky almost close enough to touch. "What're the odds of something going wrong?"

"Well, I've never done this spell with others. She's part Air Mage, so that'll make it easier. Hold on to me and hold tight to each other. Even in spirit form, you'll be able to hang on. I'll keep us together and guide us as best as I can." The big knight stepped beside Eri, right under the current.

Eri held his arm out, and Ilia dashed over. She wrapped her arm around Eri and gripped the big knight's woolen tunic with pale fingers. Eri gripped his master's belt and held Ilia tightly against his side.

Her stomach jolted and her head felt floaty. She pressed her head against Eri's side and focused on holding as firm as she could. Everything went black. Colours burst around her and rushed past. No, she was rushing past them, being carried by the current. They still had form, still looked like themselves, but were translucent, almost silhouettes of light. Was she seeing their souls, or their magical essence, or something else?

Ilia jolted again and felt her feet hit something solid. Eri pressed her to his side firmly, keeping her upright. Her knees buckled, but she didn't let go. After a few deep breaths, Ilia straightened up and looked around. They were in the mountains.

A small path led down into a valley. A dragon lay at the bottom, its side heaving with each slow breath. It hissed and belched a flame out at someone. A few large boulders hid them from the view of whoever was attacking the dragon.

Ilia scrambled up the boulders and peeked over the top. A man in the black armour walked around the dragon. Other mages stood around, back out of flaming distance. Eri and the big knight joined her. Ilia glanced at the massive man as he muttered under his breath. They dropped back from the boulders.

The big knight's armour appeared around him, shining in the sun. "Stay here and stay hidden, girl."

Eri's armour flashed over him. He nodded to Ilia. "We'll be fine. Keep behind cover and don't let them know you're here."

"Come, Eri." He drew his sword and charged around the boulder, shield raised, fireballs shooting from his sword tip.

Eri pulled his sword from the scabbard and followed his master. Ilia huddled behind the rock, peering out at the black knight. Was it the same one, or a different one? She had to help. Her friends were charging into danger. She couldn't sit here and let them get hurt.

The dragon's side heaved again, a deep rumble with each breath. Its golden eye rolled towards Ilia. She pressed her hand to her heart and gasped. Energy flowed into her, rolling and moving and energizing her in waves, matching the dragon's breath.

A fireball flew past and spattered on the rocks behind her. Ilia darted out and to another boulder closer to the dragon, keeping low in a crouch. Please, let the rock hide me, she pleaded. Let the mountains be like a forest to me.

She hurled herself behind the next boulder as lightning flashed where she just was. Ilia peeked out again. Eri shot fire from his sword, his shield reflecting lightning that the mage hurled his way. The massive knight fought three mages, his sword flashing in the sunlight and shimmering with fire.

The dragon was one more quick dash away. If she could get close, maybe she could heal it. Ilia ran from her boulder and tucked in against the dragon's side, back near its shoulders. She scurried up along the scaly neck and spines, to the creature's head.

A golden eye looked right at her. Ilia raised her hand to the dragon's nose. Power flowed through her and into the dragon, every ounce of healing she could muster. She could do this. She had to do this.

The dragon took a shallow breath, squeaking with the exhale. Her energy was fading fast. A spear had pierced her lung, and she was slipping away.

"No, please. I've never done lungs before, but I'll try," she whispered.

The scaly side rose briefly, and the dragon coughed, wheezing and rattling with the attempted breath. Ilia poured every bit of magical energy she had into the dragon. No, she was too small, the dragon too large and magical. The enormous heart slowed. All magic inside the dragon was gathering around the heart, barely beating now.

"That dragon is mine!"

Ilia spun and fell back against the hard snout, her magical connection broken. Black armour shone in the sunlight; a black spear held above her, pointed at her heart.

"You can't have her." Ilia balled her fists and pressed herself up. She stood between him and the dragon, her hands raised. Magic flared on her fingertips, just a little wisp of what she had left.

The knight laughed, his black helmet tipping back. A flash of silver cloth showed around his neck. A weak point. "I'll take that dragon. No child will stop me."

"You can't have her." Ilia wrapped her hand around the crystal, the hard ridges easy to feel through her robes. Power pulsed through her. Was it enough?

The black knight thrust the spear down. Ilia stood her ground, hand raised, her shield spell on her fingertips. She jolted as the spear passed through her shield.

"Save my babies," a voice whispered in her mind. An image of eggs and a nest flashed before her eyes.

CLANG! Ilia fell back on the rock. The spear deflected sideways, sliding off her. Ilia scrambled up to sit. The dragon was gone, completely gone, and shining iridescent white armour covered Ilia.

"You stole the dragon. I'm going to kill you." The knight charged at her, pulling his sword.

Ilia jumped to her feet and pulled the sword from her belt. The white blade reflected the light like a prism, scattering colours around her. Eri appeared at her side, sword out and facing the knight.

Knight-Master Brannon stepped between her and the black knight, sword and shield in hand. "Your followers have fled. The dragon is gone. You are under arrest for attacking the dragon. The black armour you wear is proof of other crimes against the dragons. Come and face justice."

Ilia sighed, her sword shaking as she held it out. She shifted closer to Eri and peered around the big knight.

The black knight stared at her. His glowing red eyes shone through the visor. "Some other time." He shimmered and faded.

"Where'd he go?" Eri walked to the spot the knight was moments ago. "What happened? Where's the dragon?" He turned and looked Ilia up and down.

She sheathed her sword and pulled her helmet off. "What is all this?" She looked down at herself, fully clad in the shiny white armour.

Knight-Master Brannon kneeled beside her and pulled a metal gauntlet off. He touched the helmet she held, his fingers sliding over the smooth surface. "That's dragon scale armour. He must have willed it to you with his dying breath." The big knight shimmered, and his armour disappeared.

"What? Are you sure?" Eri stepped closer and reached out. He brushed his hand over the curved horns on the helmet.

Ilia stared down at the helmet. Save her babies? She must have a nest somewhere, but where? She tried to picture that image. At first it was blurry, lacking details, but the image sharpened, like she was standing before it now.

Something pulled her to the east. The nest was over that way. She just knew it.

"We need to go back to Mithlan. I have to contact the castle as soon as possible." The big knight rose to his feet and began walking.

"Yes, Master." Eri shimmered and his armour disappeared. He glanced back at her.

"Come, girl."

Ilia stood rooted to the spot. The pull east was almost overwhelming. "I have something I need to do first."

He turned and stared at her, his frown deep. "This is more important. She was the last dragon, and now she's gone. We have black knights on the loose, and they can teleport. We need to talk to the experts as soon as possible."

Ilia shook her head. "No. She's not the last dragon."

Silence, the inner voice whispered. We're being listened to.

Ilia pressed her hand to the dragon scale breastplate over her heart. Alright.

The big knight stepped up to her. "What?"

She glanced around. "I can't explain here. When we get back, I have something important to say," she whispered.

Her armour grew warm. I am with you. You are worthy and you can save the dragons. I will help you.

Ilia closed her eyes and opened her senses. Her armour almost pulsed with life. You're alive?

In a sense. I live in you now, a part of you. Keep that secret for now.

"Are you okay?" Eri touched her cheek, pulling Ilia from her thoughts.

She blinked up at him. "Yeah, I'm just—this is so—"

"First battle where someone tried to kill you?" He smiled at her.

Ilia's knees felt weak, and her legs wanted to shake. "Yeah. It's not like in training."

The massive knight shook his head. "No, it's not, but you are brave. Let's go." He turned and started walking again.

"You're injured." Ilia reached out and took his arm in her hand, lifting it to expose a streak of red.

The big knight stood quietly as Ilia shifted the slashed tunic and checked the cut inside his arm. He held his arm still as she placed a hand on either side of the wound.

"Let me heal that. It'll only take moments."

He nodded and kneeled. Ilia poured healing magic into the wound, willing the cut to stitch itself back together. The skin closed, and the muscle fibers repaired themselves. Ilia nodded and lowered her hands from his thick upper arm.

"Thanks." The big knight unfolded his long legs and stood. "You can let your armour dissipate now. Just think 'I am safe' and it should disappear, waiting for you to call it again."

Ilia took a deep breath. Would her armour react like regular armour?

He's right, though not for the reasons he thinks. Just need me, and I'll be there. Touch the bracelet or anklet and wish for me. I'll appear and protect you. When you are safe, acknowledge me. I'll wait for you, tied to your essence, but not physically burdening you. I won't leave you.

Thank you, Ilia thought, hoping the armour could hear her. *I appreciate it.*

Her armour shimmered and faded, leaving behind thin dragon scale bands around her wrists and ankles. Her travel robes were dusty and tattered. She glanced up at the men. The big knight was looking down at her. Ilia squirmed.

"Let's go back."

Eri took her shaking hand and guided her along behind the big knight. They followed the path up, over the ridge, and down the mountain. Her body felt charged with energy, like she was well rested and had eaten recently, despite neither being true.

As she crested the ridge, she smiled. The land stretched out before her, the forest seeming to go on for miles. Rivers crossed the land, shimmering in the sunlight. The sky was a deep blue, with wispy clouds drifting on the breeze overhead. To the west she could see Mithlan, though it was too far to make out the throng of people on the roads.

What had happened, though? What magic had he used to take them right to the mountain? She'd been like a spirit, but not, flowing along a current of magic and power. There was an entire world out here, one she knew nothing about, and so much to see still. Once she was a healer, she was going to see it all.

"Is that a settlement?" Ilia pointed at the edge of the forest.

The Knight-Master nodded. "There are small outposts scattered all over the country where we can get rapid transport or send messages instantly. We can catch a wagon back to the city from there. We'll be in Mithlan before Dark."

CHAPTER 11

A SPY IN OUR MIDST

I lia stopped in the doorway. Her gaze flitted from crystal ball to water bowl to mirror, watching the mages standing over them and scrying or listening. Eri took her hand and pulled her inside. The door swung closed behind her, clicking shut quietly.

The woman stood beside the large mirror, her hand on the frame. The big knight nodded.

Something moved beside her. Ilia stopped and stared at a crystal ball on a pedestal. She peered at it, her face moving closer. Something was moving inside it. A tiny dragon poked its nose through the eggshell and crawled out. It flapped its stubby little wings. A young woman reached down and picked up the little dragon. She held it out to an incredibly old woman.

"Ilia?"

She glanced up at Knight-Master Brannon. "Huh?" Her gaze flicked to the mirror, where the King and the council mages stared down at her. She glanced back at the crystal ball, but the images were gone. The ball reflected the stand underneath.

"I've told them what happened. Tell them what you saw and experienced, starting from approaching the dragon." The big knight reached out and pulled her in front of him, facing the mirror. "Can you show them?"

"Show them?" She tilted her head back to look up at him.

"The armour."

She stared, open-mouthed. "I don't know." Her neck ached. Ilia straightened her neck and rubbed the muscles.

"Speak, child. What happened?" The King crossed his arms over his chest.

Everyone in the mirror stared at her. Ilia opened her mouth. The words got stuck in her throat. It was hard to draw a breath.

The big knight placed a warm hand on her shoulder. "Take a breath. Just go over it slowly, from when we saw the dragon."

She closed her eyes and nodded. Breathing was easier when she didn't see everyone staring at her. "I stayed hidden, away from the fighting. I could see her, though, the dragon, I mean. She called to me. Something in her eyes pulled at me. I snuck over to her." Ilia shivered. Those eyes, they were so full of pain.

"You're doing great. What happened next?" The big knight squeezed her shoulder lightly.

"I tried to help her. My healing magic wasn't enough. She was so powerful. I'd never have been enough. The black knight came. I stood between him and her. He tried to run me through with a spear. The armour appeared. His spear bounced off." Ilia wiped a tear from her cheek.

Keep my eggs a secret. It's still not safe. Someone listening is a threat.

"She was gone, just like that."

"Was there anything else you wanted to say?" the big knight prompted.

Ilia shook her head. She kept her eyes closed.

"Do you still have the armour?" Ilia knew Master Dinoc's voice.

Ilia nodded.

"You're telling me the armour was given to a girl, a student even, and not my Knight-Master in charge of my Elite Guard?"

Ilia squeezed her eyes shut. Don't cry. Please don't cry in front of everyone.

I'm with you.

"The dragons choose for their own reasons. She would know things we do not, and sense things we cannot." How does Master Dinoc know all these things? Has he read every book and scroll in the library?

"Ilia."

She knew that voice. Ilia opened her eyes. "Yes, Champion?"

The lady knight stepped closer to the mirror. "Did you get a sword with the armour? A shield?"

Ilia nodded. Her fingers brushed over the dragon scale bracelet, smooth and warm to her touch.

"That sword can pierce the black armour. It's the only thing that can, since it was imbued with the full strength of the dragon, and not stolen from one. Your weapons and armour are stronger than those the black knight have." Master Dinoc smiled at her.

"They are trained knights. What can a girl do against them? A healer, and not even a knight in training?" The King paced in front of the mirror.

"Her basics are good, Highness." The Champion smiled at Ilia. "Brannon, drill her when you can. I'll be there as soon as I'm able."

The big knight nodded. "I will."

"Knight-Master Brannon, we will meet in an hour over the mirror with the generals. You, too, Champion, before you go anywhere. I want a plan to defend the kingdom, and one that does not pin all our hopes on an untested child. Dismissed."

The reflective mirror surface turned to a dark swirling fog. Ilia balled her fists at her sides. She didn't ask for this. She never wanted this. She just wanted her friends safe.

"Eri, take her for food and make sure she rests. I'll be down after the meeting."

"Yes, Master." Eri took her hand. "Come, and no running off this time. I'm hungry, and I'm sure you'd love some tea, at least."

Her belly churned. Ilia wrapped an arm around herself. "I could use some mint tea."

Eri smiled. He pulled her gently, getting her moving. "We've got some in the pantry. I'll bring some while you rest in our rooms."

She followed him down the stairs to the second floor. It's a good thing he knows which room it is, because they all look the same to me.

He stopped at a door and opened it, revealing the familiar room inside. Ilia crossed the room and opened a window, letting the light breeze in. She let the breeze flow over her, calming her stomach. Ilia looked out at the city below her.

The brightly coloured tents and awnings gave the city a splash of colour, cheering the view up. People milled about in the streets, heading to and from the markets. Wagons rolled by. There was no noise, though. Were the windows spelled for quiet, too?

Eri leaned against the wall beside her. "Is it overwhelming, being somewhere so busy?"

Ili glanced up at him. "No. Well, yes." She squirmed at the smile. "The noise is unexpected. There're so many people here, and they're all jammed together. They kept the Healing Wing quiet so people could rest."

Eri raised his eyebrow. "They kept students quiet? How?"

Ilia laughed and shook her head. "Our living quarters were all spelled, as much so the healers could rest undisturbed as the patients. I live with Master Silvan in her personal quarters, so my room was quiet and away from any commotion the other students caused."

"I'll go get you that tea. Mint, was it?" He strode to the door and stopped, his hand on the knob.

"Yes, please."

"You can sleep on my bed if you need rest, or just relax and lie down." Eri pointed at the crisply made bed with a light blanket and cotton sheets. "I'll know if you try to leave this room, so please stay put this time, alright?"

Ilia grinned and looked down. "Sure."

Eri shook his head as he left the room. The door closed behind him.

Ilia looked around the room. The large table had maps scattered across the surface. Ilia pulled a map of the entire country over and scanned it. If the feeling was pulling her southeast, where could it be? She poured over the map, leaning closer to see the details.

Her eyes ached. Ilia straightened up and glanced about. Two beds pretty much filled the one wall with the windows. Each had a small table beside it, and both had books on top. A small bookcase stuffed with books sat near the desk. Ilia kneeled and looked at the titles. Sword and Sorcery, Battle Tactics, How to Clean Armour, and other soldier related books filled every space.

The door swung open. Eri walked in, a tray balanced in his hands. Ilia spun and stood; wide-eyed.

Eri chuckled. "You look like a startled deer."

"I do not." Ilia scowled.

"Not now. Now you look like Master Silvan. Come and eat. There's an entire pot of mint tea for you." Eri slid some maps out of the way and set the tray on the table.

He pulled the chairs closer to the tray and set the plates and cups out. Eri deftly poured tea without spilling a drop on the maps. Ilia moved over and ran her fingers over the smooth and polished chair. She smiled and sat. The fresh baking on her plate smelled sweet, and the herbed bun had all her favourite spices in it.

Eri sat in the other chair. "You didn't tell us everything, did you?" He picked up his steaming teacup and waved a finger over it. The steam dissipated, and he cradled the cup in his hands.

Ilia shook her head. She closed her eyes. Can I tell him?

"Yes, it's safe now. No one is listening, and he might help.

Ilia opened her eyes. She picked up the herbed bun. "The dragon has a nest. She has eggs. Dragons still exist, and I promised her I'd find the eggs and protect them."

Eri's mouth dropped open. His teacup clattered against the table as he set it down. "Why didn't you tell us?"

"Well—" Ilia's stomach churned. She set her bun down and picked up her teacup. "The dragon still talks to me. She warned me someone dangerous was listening in during the mirror call, and when she first transformed, she told me that place wasn't safe to talk. I've been waiting for her to say I could tell you."

"We need to tell Master."

"I know. As soon as she tells me it's safe, I plan to. I need to find the nest, though." Ilia sipped the tea. The mint refreshed her mouth and calmed her stomach. "I need to find the nest."

"She talks to you?" Eri tore his roll apart and stuffed some in his mouth.

"It's like I hear her in my mind. I can talk to her, and ask her things, and she answers me." Ilia nibbled a little piece of her roll.

"That's—pretty amazing, actually. Did she tell you where the nest was?"

Ilia shook her head. "She tried to show me. I feel something pulling me towards it. I can find it, but I don't really know how far it is, how I'll get there, or even how I'll protect the eggs once I find them."

Eri wiped crumbs from his tunic. He picked up his teacup and swirled the tea gently around. "Well, that's alright, then. At least we have a direction. You've been looking?" He nodded at the map. "You moved it."

Ilia's cheeks burned. He noticed? She nodded. "I was hoping to see some marking or something, a mountain in the right direction, maybe. I'm not that skilled with maps, though."

"Finish your food and we'll look together. I'm an expert with maps. We might narrow it down a bit."

***

Eri leaned over the map, now centered on the table. The empty plates and tray sat by the door, out of the way. "You said southeast?"

Ilia nodded. She could feel his warmth, standing here beside him, almost touching. "I feel pulled that way." She pointed at a wall.

"Okay, that's a little more east than southeast, so if we follow that on the map," his finger brushed over the smooth paper, "that'll put us about—here. That doesn't make sense. It's all forest and grasslands until we reach the eastern mountain range."

Ilia frowned. "That's a long way to go. The image I saw, though, it wasn't jagged peaks, but more hills or something."

"Hills. That gives us some possibilities, now. Here, just south of the forest in the foothills, here near the lakes, and here, but that's a little off the direction you said." Eri pointed on the map at each spot. "It narrows it down, though."

The door swung open, and Knight-Master Brannon appeared, filling the doorway. He noticed them at the map and stepped beside them, towering over Ilia. "What's got you two so fascinated with the map?"

Eri looked at Ilia and raised an eyebrow.

Ilia closed her eyes. Can I tell him?

113

Yes, he's safe. This room is protected.

Ilia opened her eyes. She nodded to Eri.

"The dragon has eggs. Ilia promised to find them and protect them." Eri shared everything Ilia had told him with his master, and how they were investigating the map.

The big knight frowned. "Someone on the council, she said?"

"Maybe." Ilia squirmed under his piercing gaze. "Someone listening in. Maybe in the room with us, like the woman running the mirrors, or at the castle. She didn't know exactly who."

The big knight rubbed his temples and sauntered to the window. "She. Your armour talks to you. What else can she do?"

Ilia opened her mouth. She closed it again and thought for a moment. "I don't know yet."

He nodded slowly, his gaze down on the map. "You're going after the eggs?"

"I have to," Ilia whispered. "I promised. They need protecting."

"Now, I take it you two have some idea where to look, with how intently you were staring at the map. Athia is a big place, you know." The big knight walked over and gestured to the map.

"Hills. Somewhere southeast of here. That way." Ilia pointed again.

"That's what we've got to go on? Hills, that way? Eri, what are your thoughts?" He leaned over the map, his hands on the table.

Ilia shifted and gave him room. She listened as they talked about the places Eri thought were most promising. Were they going to help her?

"If it's along this line, maybe here." Eri traced the path with his finger.

"That's still a lot of possibilities. While those are the least inhabited hills on the path, it's still a large area to search. We'll need camping supplies. Start packing. I'll get things for her to use. She can carry her own pack. We're camping wild, so pack accordingly." The big knight straightened up and left the room.

CHAPTER 12

HEADING OUT

"Thank you." Ilia touched Eri's arm. "I thought I'd have to sneak out and go alone."

Eri snorted. "I doubt you could sneak away again." He grinned at her. "I'm pretty sure he's afraid of Master Silvan. Most knights are. He promised to protect you and get you back to the castle."

Ilia stared at him. "Afraid of her? Really?" Her hand fell away.

Eri nodded. He walked to his bed and pulled his pack out from under it. "Really. You think injured knights willingly lay in bed when their friends are in danger? She's terrified nearly all of them into resting at some point, and he's known her longer than most." He rifled through his pack.

Ilia pressed a hand to her mouth and tried to hide her grin. "She can be rather—intimidating, I guess. Maybe I'm used to it."

Eri took some things out and tossed them in the trunk. He pulled some clothing from the trunk and tucked them in the pack. "You're not nearly as intimidated by Master as most people. I'll give you that."

Ilia giggled. "I'm shaking on the inside." She sat on the bed beside his pack.

Eri smiled. "I honestly couldn't tell."

She shrugged. "As healers, we're trained to look confident and act brave, even when we're falling apart inside. It helps the most seriously injured patients recover when they might otherwise have died."

The big knight returned, a small pack in his hand. He held it up for her. "Come try it on, and I'll help you adjust the straps."

Ilia stood and walked over to him. She smiled to herself. It was easy to see why people were intimidated by him, even though he'd only been good to her. She wriggled an arm under each strap, and he let the pack hang from her shoulders.

"You tighten the straps like this." He kneeled in front of her and adjusted a buckle. "These two bring the pack up higher, and these two hold it closer to you."

Ilia smiled. "It's a lot like the herb collection bags we use. Just a bit heavier and thicker."

The big knight nodded. "Same design, but a bit more rugged. Is it too heavy for you?"

Ilia chuckled. "No. Ask me again after we've been walking all day, though."

He grinned at her. The big knight stood and went for his own pack. "I got us a wagon ride to an outpost. You can rest on the way, and we'll spend the night there. We'll set off on foot in the morning. Eri, are you packed?"

"Yes, Master." Eri picked up his pack and slid his arms through the straps.

The big knight left the room, Ilia and Eri behind him. Her pack bumped against the doorframe when she turned down the hall. It was light enough, but bigger than the collection packs she was used to. Ilia moved to the middle of the hallway, right behind the large man. Eri walked behind her, his footsteps silent.

She gripped the railing going down the stairs. Everything seemed small, like the walls were closing in. She couldn't see around the large man, and he blocked much of the light. Ilia took slow breaths and focused on each step. It seemed too long when she finally emerged back into the light on the main floor.

Ilia swung wide around the door frame. Her pack hit the desk. "Drat it all," she muttered under her breath.

"It gets easier," Eri whispered, his hand on her pack as he helped her through the door.

A wagon stood on the street, supplies in crates under a tarp in half the back part. It had gigantic wheels and was raised higher than carriages. It must go cross-country, or through fields, she thought, as she looked at the varnished and shining wood.

The big knight stopped beside the wagon and set his pack in the back. "Take your pack off and I'll put it up for you. Climb in."

Ilia slipped the straps from her shoulders and the pack hit the cobblestones. She winced at the metallic clinking as her pack landed. Hopefully, there's nothing breakable in there, just the metal dishes. Ilia wrinkled her brow. She had no idea what was in her pack.

He lifted her pack in for her with one hand. She wriggled up into the wagon, using the small steps and pressing up with both hands to wiggle into the back. Eri tossed his pack in. It landed with the same clinking, and Ilia smiled. Eri leapt up and landed beside her. The big knight walked to the front of the wagon and stepped up into the control seat beside the driver, his long legs letting him climb with ease.

"We strap the packs in like this." Eri slid the three packs against the side of the wagon and pulled a strap around them. "Now they're secure if we get jostled on the road, though we usually have a smooth ride."

Ilia leaned close and examined the wide woven strap. It had metal buckles that clamped down in place and held securely.

Eri moved closer to the front of the wagon, next to the crates, and leaned back against the side. He patted the wagon floor beside him. Ilia crawled over and sat between him and the packs. The driver glanced at them and lifted the back board into place. The wagon shook as the latches locked. Eri stretched his arm along the side of the wagon and Ilia leaned her head back against him.

The wagon shook as the driver climbed into his control seat. "Ready back there?"

"Ready," Eri called.

The wagon started rolling. Ilia bumped against the packs. Eri dropped his arm around her and pulled her close. Ilia curled up against him. The wagon rolled towards the city gate, the crowd parting for it and closing behind once it passed.

She glanced out the back as they rolled along. A dirty child stared back at her, tucked in the shadows of a building. That could have been her, if Master Silvan hadn't taken her in. In a couple of years, he'd be old enough to start magic training with a master or in a school. What would happen to him then?

She closed her eyes and let her head rest against Eri's chest. City noises slowly faded behind her. If this is what cities were like, she didn't want to see another for a long time. Everyone talks about how great things are, but not for everyone, apparently. Wasn't anything being done for those who had nothing?

The wagon smoothed out as the road switched from stone to packed dirt. The gentle swaying was soothing, like being rocked to sleep.

***

"This way."

Ilia followed the big knight from the dining hall. The outpost was more comfortable than the city was, much smaller and made of wood instead of stone. She'd fallen asleep on the wagon, not waking until they arrived. They stopped in the dining hall first, and Ilia happily tried the new foods there, all quick snacks to give energy for the knights. Their packs were still in the dining hall. Where were they going?

The big knight walked over to a sandy training ring between two of the outpost buildings. Wooden training dummies stood just beyond the sand, ready for sword practice. Ilia glanced up at Eri beside her. Eri was smiling and looked a lot more awake than she felt.

Knight-Master Brannon stopped in the middle of the sand ring. "Call up your armour, girl." His armour formed around his body.

Ilia sighed. Didn't he know her name? She brushed her fingers over the dragon scale bracelet. Armour, can you come, please? The air around her shimmered. Her armour appeared, the weight resting on her shoulders and body like a hug, not like the closed and sweaty feel of the borrowed leather armour she was used to.

"Did Champion Loni teach you how to use a shield?" He eyed the shield strapped to her back.

Ilia shook her head. "Only the sword. We didn't get to shields yet."

"Well, we'll start now. The more practice you get, the better. Do you know how to hold a shield?"

Well, sort of, she thought. I've seen it done. She'd even helped the Champion into her armour and given her a shield, so how hard could it be? Ilia pulled her shield around. It looked the same on the back, a handle and some straps. Ilia slid her arm under the straps and gripped the handle. The straps snugged down on her arm. The shield felt lighter than the metal ones in the armoury.

"For a shield to work, it has to be in the right place. Hold it up like this." He pulled his shield onto his arm and held it up in front of his body, slightly to one side. "Make sure there's space between you and your shield. If it's right against your body, you'll feel every blow. One good hit could send you flying." He turned sideways so he could show her.

Ilia lifted her arm and raised her shield. Within moments, her shoulder muscles protested being in one position with a weight on her arm. Her grip slipped on the handle and her shield rotated on her arm. Ilia shifted her grip and straightened her shield.

"Keep the arm up and your grip snug. Not tight, but enough to prevent that shifting. The shield won't protect you if it doesn't cover you."

She firmed her grip and raised her arm. The shield knocked against her shins. Her leg armour protected her. Ilia changed her grip again. Maybe this time? Her shield steadied in her grip, and she smiled.

"Now, your shield angle matters, and you can change it to defend you better. If you're facing an acid attack, angle it down slightly like this." He stood beside her and showed her. "The acid will splash down and away, hopefully towards the attacker. Be mindful of where the land slopes."

"Wait, are acid attacks likely?" She narrowed her eyes at Eri.

Eri grinned at her and picked up a wooden sword.

"Likely enough. If we're facing black knights, you need to watch for fire attacks. They'll have a boost to their fire magic, from their armour and stolen powers."

Ilia stared up at the big knight, wide-eyed.

"Acid is more an army thing, as you can get a lot of men at once with it." Eri raised his wooden sword.

"With fire, angle the shield up slightly. Flames will rise above you, harmlessly deflected into the sky. If you do it right, it'll bounce flames into the air, away from you and your allies. Like this." The big knight tilted his shield.

Ilia turned her forearm and her shield shifted in her grip as it tilted up like his. Flames spattered her shield and Ilia squeaked, her legs shaking as she ducked behind her shield.

The flames stopped, and she poked her head out, glaring at Eri. "I wasn't ready."

"Your attacker won't wait for you to be ready." The big knight sighed. "They'll attack when you're unprepared or not focused. Stand fast and he'll hit you with a good burst. Keep that shield up and you won't burn to death."

Flames smacked her shield and burst around her. Ilia curled up behind her shield as the fire bounced up into the sky.

I won't let you burn.

Ilia blinked. She felt the connection with her armour, felt the reassurances in her heart. "Thank you," she whispered.

The flames stopped. Ilia remained frozen behind her shield, sweat beading on her skin. Oh, for a gambeson under her armour, or even thicker robes. More layers would protect her better, right?

"You can stand, girl."

Ilia peeked out around her shield. Eri stood calmly, wooden sword down by his side, smiling at her. She straightened her legs and stood. Her legs shook.

The big knight shook his head. "We'll keep practicing that until you don't even blink at it anymore. However, you also need to know how to block physical attacks. Eri?"

Eri grinned and raised his wooden sword. He wouldn't hurt her, right?

***

Ilia eased herself into the warm water. She smiled at the delicate lavender scent. Someone added the rejuvenating bath powder for her. Her skin tingled lightly with the herbs and oils. Ilia leaned against the sloping back and sank down until only her head was above the water, with her legs bent and supporting her from sliding under completely.

The outpost was small, with a few buildings, including a warehouse and the training area. It was warm, and the people were friendly. Camping in tents wasn't what she expected at all. It was more—rustic. This, though, she smiled. This was just fine, thanks. Maybe one day she'd have a cabin in the woods. She'd have her own bathroom like this, wooden floors and walls and a big metal tub. She could have a massive herb garden right outside her door.

A knock sounded on her door. Ilia jumped, splashing the water as she bolted upright.

"There's a supper tray on the table for you," Eri called, his voice slightly muffled by the wooden door.

"Thanks."

"You're welcome. Get an early night. We leave at first light."

"Alright."

She settled back against the tub, the warm metal against her muscles. Ilia filled her lungs with air and sank below the water. The water closed over her head, and she settled on the smooth tub bottom. She waited until her lungs started aching. Her head broke the surface and water cascaded down her body as she sat.

Ilia leaned back and watched the water ripple around her knees. She called a little ball of water together and it rose from the bath, going wherever her finger pointed. Ilia bounced the water across the surface a few times before she let it go. The little ball returned to the bathwater with a splash.

Her stomach growled and her belly twinged. Travelling should involve more snacking. At least she had the snack before the training session, though with all the energy she burned, it wasn't near enough for her liking. Her muscles were relaxed again. Ilia smiled. She might even have helped design this herbal bath blend with Master Silvan and the other healers. It sure smelled familiar.

She rose from the water. Ilia snapped her fingers, and the bathwater fell away, leaving her dry. She held the tall side of the tub and stepped out onto the thick wool bathmat. Ilia lifted her nose and sniffed. She could smell the stew over the light smell of lavender, strong culinary herbs that made her mouth water. Ilia finished drying herself and pulled her borrowed cotton bathrobe on.

Ilia plopped herself into the chair at the small table and picked up her spoon. She wolfed down the thick stew loaded full of chunks of vegetables and gulped her apple juice down. Her eyelids threatened to slam shut as she set her spoon beside her empty bowl. Ilia wandered to the bed and collapsed, pulling the covers over herself as her head hit the pillow.

CHAPTER 13

UNEXPECTED ALLIES

The sun was barely peeking over the horizon when a large hand shook her awake. Ilia stumbled through her morning routine and packing up. Everyone was silent as they ate, though the knights looked far too perky for this early hour. Eri helped her get her pack on, and they headed out into the forest. After walking for hours, Ilia finally felt awake.

"How do you do that?" Ilia stared at the small leaf, levitating just above the big knight's hand. It floated freely and pointed in the direction they headed.

"It's a compass spell. I hold a picture in my mind of what I'm looking for, or where I'm heading, or even a direction. This time, I'm focused on the direction you showed me on the map. The leaf will point in that direction any time I hold it out. Try it. Find a leaf with a definite point. Slender leaves work better."

Ilia scanned the forest floor. It was too early for most leaves to have turned or fallen, but a few damaged branches scattered the forest floor. Ilia selected a leaf from one and plucked it free. She held it up in her palm.

"Now, say these words and picture what you want." The big knight taught her a chant, letting her repeat it until she got it, which didn't take long.

She imagined the nest as the dragon showed it to her and chanted softly. The leaf rose from her palm an inch and turned to point in the direction they walked. It matched the big knight's leaf.

"That's a good sign. We'll have a fast lunch and be on our way."

Ilia sighed as she settled on the grass. She stretched her legs out as the knight portioned out their meal. Everyone ate quietly, and they were on their way again. Within a couple of hours, way too many hours of walking for her taste, she saw something through the trees.

She smiled and sped up, walking past the big knight. A large lake stretched out before her, the sun shining down on the water and grassy banks where the trees didn't block the light. The land beyond grabbed her attention, just past the forest.

"That's it. That's where the nest is." Ilia pointed at the hilltops ahead of them.

Knight-Master Brannon followed her gaze. "We'll be there tomorrow at this pace. You're sure?"

"I'm certain. That's what she showed me."

They stopped for a drink and a quick supper before heading out again. It wasn't far to the edge of the forest now, and the hills were just beyond. With her destination in sight, Ilia relaxed and looked around as they walked.

Small animals darted around, looking for food, little mice and squirrels, and more. Birds flitted about and chirped, heading back to their nests after a day of foraging. She noticed the edible herbs everywhere, it seemed. This part of the forest was full of abundance. It helped keep her mind from her tired legs.

"We'll camp here. Quick camp, no tent. It's a warm night." The big knight lowered his pack to the ground.

"I'll get some herbs for the meal." Ilia dropped her pack to the grass.

The big knight made a quick firepit, but instead of a fire, a magical flame burned in the middle. Eri helped Ilia gather some berries and herbs. She handed the bounty to the big knight, who mixed them into their rations. Ilia watched him tend the magical flame with finger motions, warming or cooling the heat as he needed. Could she learn to do the same?

With supper eaten and their campsite tidied, Ilia tucked herself into her bedroll. The stars twinkled above her, shining brightly without the moon up yet to hide their light. She saw so much new magic today. Would she get to learn more? Master Silvan concentrated her education on healing spells, but the world was so much bigger and more diverse than she imagined. What else would she discover out here? Was a lifetime enough to see it all?

She rolled onto her side and closed her eyes. Her legs were tired, but she still felt the oils and herbs from the bath. Would it last the entire trip, or was she going to be sore tomorrow? How did the knights do it, all the walking?

Gentle splashes got her attention. Eri was beside her, already lightly snoring, so it must be the Knight-Master. He had a pot of fresh lake water, and must be washing up, from the sound of it. Ilia shivered. That had to be cold. No, anyone smart would warm the water with magic. She would have.

She reached up and pressed on her makeshift pillow, her folded travel cloak, and sighed. Too tired to care about her lack of creature comforts, Ilia let herself drift off.

Ilia flew through the sky, the land disappearing behind her swiftly as she flapped her mighty wings. The land was a vibrant green below her, thick forest as far as she could see from her low height. Mighty trees poked above the leafy canopy, and Ilia dodged them and kept flying. Moonlight glimmered off the lake she passed. She glanced up to see the stars above, glowing against the dark sky.

The castle was in the distance, tall towers with banners flapping in the breeze. Lights brightened the southwestern sky, as if Mithlan was a beacon calling all traders in. Far to the west, Dinlark guarded the border. Tiny lights moved about, the guards on patrol on the city walls. Only her sharp dragon-like vision let her pick them from the blackness, especially at this distance.

She turned northeast, speeding over the massive central forest. Ilia followed the river that cut through the trees. The middle of the forest caught her eye, nearly glowing with magic. Wait, she could see magic, if she focused. The land was full of it. She exhaled it with every breath.

A cluster of trees in the middle of the forest shimmered with magic. Ilia sped towards them, tall and bright, strong and vibrant. The trees were older here. She could sense it somehow. She spied a break in the canopy, near the very middle of the forest, where a single tree was visible just above the others.

Her wings folded and Ilia touched down on the soft grass. She stared up at the tree with her human eyes, the tree rising high above her now human form. The other trees stood back from this one, like they wouldn't dare try to grow any closer. Soft moss covered the damp soil between the roots.

The long branches swayed in the breeze, stretching wide over the clearing and hanging down. The gentle swaying was almost hypnotic. This tree looked different, with a gnarled trunk of rich brown and leaves so green they almost glowed. Tender blossoms peeked out between leaves.

A woman stepped out from behind the trunk. "Come, child." She opened her arms to Ilia.

Ilia took slow steps towards her. Her smile was welcoming, and her bright green eyes looked just like Ilia's, except Ilia's were light grey. The woman's skin was the same rich brown as the tree trunk, and her hair was bright green like the leaves. Ilia could barely take her eyes off the woman. If her dragon senses were still active, would the woman glow with magic? Something about this woman felt familiar.

"Mother?" Ilia's jaw dropped open.

The woman smiled wider. "Yes, child. I need to talk to you."

Ilia dashed over, stumbling on the roots. She stretched her hand out and caught herself on the tree trunk. The woman wrapped her arms around Ilia and held her close. She lowered to the soft moss, taking Ilia with her, and sat with Ilia in her arms.

"I'm sorry I need to ask for your help, but you can do things the others can't. You're special." Brown fingers brushed over Ilia's forehead tenderly and tucked a lock of Ilia's wild hair behind her ear.

"They?" Ilia blinked up at her mother. Her mother was a tree. Should that bother her?

"The other children of the soil, child. Mages. They are special and I love them, but they aren't like you. You are my direct offspring, my first daughter conceived from a human man. There's more of me in you than you knew."

Ilia swallowed. Her throat felt tight. "How can I help?" Questions swirled inside her brain, but that one came out first.

"My other children, my children of the skies, they're in danger. You know this. You seek the last of them now. One has already gifted you with the weapons and tools you need to save them. You'll need more help to succeed."

Ilia brushed her fingers over the bracelet on her left wrist. "I'm not sure how I'm going to do this, or even fully what to do," she whispered.

"You can do this. Be their guardian. Gather the eggs and take them south, to a place I've prepared for them. There's an island with a cave. Seal them inside with this." The woman pulled a vial from her robes and tucked it into Ilia's hand. "It'll open when the time is right. You'll know what to do."

"How will I find the island?" Ilia gazed up at her mother's bright eyes. Her own eyes slid closed, her body growing heavy. Was she tired in a dream? This was a dream, wasn't it?

"You'll know. You'll feel it, and you'll have help."

The forest swirled around her, and Ilia pressed her eyelids tightly closed. Her stomach lurched. Ilia sat up, her chest heaving with each breath. She pressed a hand to her chest and glanced down at a vial tucked in her fingers, the contents glowing a pale green.

"Ilia, are you okay?" Eri bolted upright and crawled from his bedroll.

"I'm okay." Ilia took a slow breath. There, that was better, now another.

"What's that?" Eri nodded at her hand.

Knight-Master Brannon sat up and shimmied from his bedroll. Eri kneeled beside her and cradled her hand in his. Her fingers clenched, tight and aching. Her hand started shaking. Eri pried her fingers open and the little vial fell into her lap. He rubbed her fingers, and the ache eased. She picked up the vial and held it up to the moonlight. The liquid inside glowed brighter.

"I got it in my dream," she whispered. "It sounds crazy, but it's real."

The big knight kneeled on her other side. He peered at the liquid. "Do you know what it is?"

"Sort of? I'm supposed to know how to use it when it's time. It's for sealing the eggs behind a protective barrier." Ilia frowned at the little vial.

The liquid swirled slowly, like a thick oil of as many shades of green as she could imagine. She couldn't see through it at all.

"If it's important, keep it somewhere safe. Can you get more sleep?"

Ilia looked up at the big knight. She nodded. Her body felt refreshed, not a hint of soreness despite all the walking, but she could easily sleep more.

"Good. Tuck that away and sleep. We get up early and leave at first light."

She stared at the liquid for a long moment. The vial was thick, like crystal. Ilia tucked it in her inside pocket near her heart and buttoned the pocket closed. She curled up in her blankets and closed her eyes.

***

Rustling pulled Ilia from her sleep. She opened her eyes, rested and alert. The big knight was rolling up his bedroll. She sat up and stretched. The little vial still rested in her pocket, heavy for its small size. Ilia glanced over at Eri, sleeping beside her. She touched her forehead, the memory of her mother's touch still lingering on her skin. She nodded to the big man and eased from her bedroll.

He poked Eri, and the young man rolled over. Ilia gathered some herbs and took some rations, watching as the knight nudged his apprentice again. Eri sat up, hands raised in front of him, ready to strike.

"Up, Eri. Even the sleepy girl is almost ready to leave," the Knight-Master teased.

She served breakfast, and they ate quietly in the silence. The sun wasn't up yet, though the earliest hints of purples and pinks were just visible through the leaves. Bedrolls were packed, dishes were cleaned, and they were on their way.

The big knight led the way through the trees. She followed between him and Eri, a bounce in her step. After flying last night in her dream, she had so much energy running through her body, it felt like she could fly again. Midday came and went, and she still felt ready for anything. The edge of the forest was just ahead. She could feel it. How, though, and why?

She pressed her hands over her ears, wincing from the pain. What was that screeching? She glanced at Eri through the tears in her eyes. He looked pale, ready to be sick, but he held himself upright. Knight-Master Brannon shimmered, and his armour appeared. He drew his sword and held it out towards the noise. Ilia's armour appeared, not waiting for a summons. Where'd her pack go?

I've stored it where I normally wait for you, her armour assured her. When you dismiss me, it will come back.

Eri pulled her down behind the nearest bushes. "Stay in the trees. They can't attack from the air with the branches in the way."

"They?" she whispered. "They, what?"

CHAPTER 14

NOT JUST DRAGONS

"Griffins," the big knight muttered. "They're fast, so don't take any chances. Stay close."

She drew her sword. Ilia shifted her shield onto her arm. Hopefully, those lessons were enough. A flash of gold through the trees drew her eye. Something passed over the canopy and was gone, faster than a blink. The trees shook. Something big was coming.

"Come out, girl. We want to talk."

Ilia shivered. She tightened her grip on her sword. There was nothing she wanted to say to that voice. He could take his spear and shove—

"She's not interested," Knight-Master Brannon called back. "Talk to me instead." His fingers wiggled, and he muttered a spell. "It's just the black knight and two griffins." He kept his voice low.

"Just, he says," Eri mumbled. "That's enough, Master."

"We can do this. I'll handle the black knight, keep him busy, with the griffin he's riding. You keep her safe from the other griffin. You're ready."

Ilia glanced between the knights. "Are we better hiding, or waiting, or something?"

"We have to cross the open fields to get into the hills. We can face them now or later." The Knight-Master pulled his shield from his back to his arm. "I'll cast glamours and create multiple versions of us. With luck, the knight won't know who to attack. If the griffins are visual hunters, they might also fall for it. If their sense of smell is good, we might still be in trouble."

"Master, with all due respect," Eri folded his arms over his chest. "That's a terrible plan."

"I'd love to hear a better one." The big knight stared down at Eri.

Eri dropped his gaze and shook his head. "How will we know which of us is real?"

"I'll know you two through my magic." The big knight sighed. "Ilia, keep your eyes on Eri. The real Eri. Don't lose him. This'll get chaotic, but you two run for the hills and stay together."

"I'm waiting." The black knight sounded annoyed, and Ilia smiled.

"We're coming out," the big knight called back. "Ready, kids?"

Ilia stayed as still as she could with her knees shaking. The big knight chanted softly. Images shimmered all around her, multiple versions of them standing around. Ilia stared around at them all, the images mirroring her movements. Oh, drat, which one's Eri? Please let this be him. He was standing right beside her.

"Let's go." The big knights all spoke in unison, the voice sounding from all around her.

"This is weird," the many versions of Eri muttered.

Focus on Eri, Ilia reminded herself. I know where I'm going. I can feel it. I can do this. She glanced up at the Eri beside her and saw movement in her peripheral vision. All the Ilia's glanced at the nearest Eri. Eri smiled at her. Ilia gave her head a shake. This was mind bending.

"Once we're through the trees, run." The big knights all turned and marched through the trees.

Ilia slipped a hand into Eri's and felt his gauntlet. Good, that's the real one. They approached the edge of the trees. A black knight sat on a griffin in the open field, the other griffin beside him.

The big knights charged from the trees, swords swinging, all yelling a battle cry that made Ilia's legs shake.

"This way," Eri whispered, tugging on her hand.

They ran into the fields and all the images of them scattered. Some ran across the fields, others through the swarm of big knights going at the griffins, and others in random directions. Ilia pushed herself faster, running hand in hand with Eri towards the hills.

She glanced back at the circle of knights around the griffins, all charging in and attacking, only to dart back again. How much energy was he burning through? Which one was really him? If he was wounded, would they all bleed? The knights ran in a tangle and formed a new circle, and she had no idea where the real Knight-Master was now.

Ilia stumbled and dropped to a knee. Eri pulled her up and kept going, letting Ilia use his arm for support. The screeching was terrible, but she didn't dare put her hands over her ears. Ilia gritted her teeth and kept running.

He guided her over the first rise and behind some boulders. She glanced back, but couldn't see the battle. Was he okay? How long would his illusion last? Her lip quivered. If he died trying to keep her safe, how would she live with that? Eri pulled her on, over the next rise, and behind more cover.

"What about him?" Her knees gave out, and she collapsed on the grass. Ilia blinked back tears.

Eri stopped and kneeled beside her. He smiled and gave her hand a squeeze. "He'll be along in moments. We need to keep going. He'll find us."

"Eri, how can he survive that? Won't he be killed?" Her throat felt tight, and her voice cracked.

"Nope, he'll be fine. Come on." Eri pulled her up and wrapped an arm around her.

Ilia stumbled on the rocks in the soil. I wish I had his confidence. She skidded and Eri held her up, not breaking stride for a moment.

"One more hill and we can rest. You can do this."

She bit back a whimper and pushed herself on. At least her armour protected her from the rocks, too. Her knees ached, but she could soothe that soon enough. Ilia clung to Eri and forced her legs to keep moving.

"Wait, that there, it's familiar." Ilia pointed between two hills, just off to their left. "That way."

Eri changed direction, staying in the lower areas and using what cover they could find. He half-carried her to a large cluster of boulders and tucked her down partially under an overhang. "We can wait here."

Ilia leaned back against the rock in the shade. Her sides ached with each breath. Ilia focused within herself and muttered the slow healing spell, her hand moving over her knees. The pain eased gradually. Some slow breaths helped her to breathe easier, and her muscles relaxed.

She strained to hear any sounds other than their own breathing. The grass rustled in the breeze. Was Eri's confidence in his master misplaced? Did he make it, or was his broken body laying on the field back there?

A griffin screeched in the distance, the sound still making her bones ache.

The ground rolled and shifted near them. Ilia pressed her hands against the rock and steadied herself. An earth-quake? Here? She glanced at Eri, who grinned back at her. The rocks beside their hiding place bubbled up like hot water, spilling down onto the grass just down the hill. The ground opened, and a hole appeared.

A hand reached up from the hole and felt around. Ilia squeaked and pressed herself back against the rock. Eri wrapped an arm around her shoulders and pulled her to his side. How was he so dratted relaxed? The dusty figure rose from the hole.

"What?" Ilia pointed a shaking finger at the massive dirt-covered knight rising from the hole. "He just—how?"

Eri took her hand and gave it a squeeze. "Easy, now. Slow and deep breaths. We'll explain once you're calm."

She stared at the big knight, wide-eyed, as he shifted under the low overhang with them and sat beside her. "I found this artifact years ago. It lets a single mage tunnel short distances through soil and some types of rock. I've been saving it for an emergency."

He held a small pendant out to her. Ilia took the pendant in a shaking hand and looked at the little circle of metal, inscribed with a fist holding a hammer, with a spell written around the edge.

"I powered it with these crystals. With the additional power, I could tunnel into the soil as far as I needed. Once below the surface, I headed for the abandoned mines in these hills. A shaft came close enough to you two that I used my last crystal and emerged right there."

The big knight held an empty crystal out to her. When full, these would glow with a bright white light. This one was completely empty, drained of its own natural energy as well. It was as good as glass now and would never work again.

"These are so rare." Ilia took the crystal and held it out into the light. The light reflected out in the colours of the rainbow on the rocky debris left from the hole.

"They keep most in the castle, for knights to take on missions like this." The big knight nodded. "I always carry one, often more than one. Our jobs are easier when our opponents aren't magically enhanced, and if they are, we can match them with the crystals. These gave me just enough power to get away. I can't protect you if I'm dead, now, can I?"

Thank you, armour, Ilia thought. Her armour shimmered and faded, leaving her in her travel robes. Her pack appeared on her back, shoving her forwards away from the

145

rock. Eri dismissed his own armour before crawling over to his master and removing his helmet. Ilia suppressed her gasp. His face was lined, and his eyes had dark shadows under them. How much energy did he use?

The big knight smiled. "I'll be fine. We'll rest and have a snack and go after that."

Ilia crawled over to the hole and looked down inside. It got black quickly and didn't seem to have an end. How deep was it? She sunk into her powers and felt the ground below her. She sensed the mine shafts crossing through the hills, felt the new tunnels he made while escaping. Wow!

The big knight downed two energy bars Eri unwrapped for him. He looked better already. Ilia took a bar for herself and chewed on the sweet, dried fruits and nuts. She felt a rush of energy through her body. Ilia tucked her wrapper into her pack.

"Alright, let's get moving." The big knight crawled from their hiding spot and stood. He moved better again, maybe not with a bounce in his step, but she no longer feared for his safety. He dismissed his armour and his pack reappeared.

Eri followed and offered Ilia his hand. She unfolded her legs and stood. Her knees no longer ached at all, and she was ready to go. The bruises would disappear over a few hours, thanks to her slow healing spell.

"This way?" Eri checked.

Ilia nodded. They wound their way up the hill, keeping close to the cover of the boulders and rocky outcroppings. The hill was steep. Her legs burned by the time they crested the rise. She looked down and gasped.

Below them, just down the hill, the rock had been burned away and a bowl-shaped area was carved out. Grasses packed down into a nest, with small branches giving it shape. She leaned over to get a better look and tumbled down. Ilia curled into a ball.

She landed on the soft grasses. The air fled her lungs, but she was unhurt.

"Ilia, are you okay?"

She lay still for a moment and checked in with herself. Limbs all still work. Nothing hurts, really. "I'm okay. We found it."

"We're coming," the big knight called.

Ilia shifted to her knees, rolling slowly. The deep grasses sank under her weight, threatening to tip her over again. She couldn't see over the edge of the nest from here, and the other side seemed so far away. She stared down into the middle of the nest. It was empty. Where were the eggs?

She pressed her hands to her temples. The pounding in her head overwhelmed her. The dragon roared inside her, howling with heartbreak. Were her bones going to rattle apart? She barely sensed Eri beside her, almost didn't feel his hand on her shoulder.

"Ilia!" Eri sounded like a distant echo.

She blinked up at Eri, her eyes open just a slit. His lips were moving, but she couldn't hear him. Eri wrapped his arms around her and clung to her.

I promise we'll find them. I won't stop looking, she whispered inside her head.

The howling quieted. Her head stopped pounding. Ilia slumped against Eri. She took slow and deep breaths, deeper each time, until she could breathe without pain or gasping. Ilia let her hands fall from her head.

"Are you okay?" Eri shifted her in his arms and peered into her eyes.

She nodded, her body still shivering. "I am. Eri, they're gone. How are we supposed to find them now? What if they've been taken somewhere, so the black knights can breed the dragons for their armour and scales?"

Knight-Master Brannon kneeled in the middle of the nest, where the faint imprints of eggs could still be seen in the grasses. He looked around and held a hand up, his fingers moving as he chanted and cast spells. "We're not alone. Stay alert."

"It's time to get rid of you, once and for all, pesky child."

Ilia whipped around. She clung to Eri. A black knight stood on the rock above the nest, his black sword in his hand. He leapt down into the nest and stalked towards her.

CHAPTER 15

PUT TO THE TEST

"**M**aster." Eri pointed behind them.

A griffin folded its wings and sped down towards them, another knight on its back.

"Guard her." The big knight turned and faced the knight on the griffin.

Eri stood and drew his sword, his armour flashing around him. He swung his shield around onto his arm. "Come no closer, murderer."

"Give us the girl and you can leave, unharmed." The black knight stepped closer. His voice echoed from his helmet.

"What do you want with her?"

"We don't want her, just her armour." His red eyes fixed on Ilia.

Eri raised his sword. "You can't have her, or her armour."

Swords clashed, metal on metal behind her. Ilia glanced back. Knight-Master Brannon and the black knight swirled around each other, swords flashing in the sun. She stood and drew her sword, turning back to the knight advancing on her. Ilia shifted her shield and held it up. Time to see what she can do.

The knight laughed. "You think you can best a trained warrior, little girl? Go ahead and try."

"Stay back," Eri warned.

The knight charged. Eri swung his sword around and attacked, his blade spinning in from all directions. His sword bounced off the armour without leaving a scratch. Eri shot flames from his sword. The fire deflected from the black breastplate and landed in the grassy nest.

"You can't hurt me." The knight turned to Ilia, ignoring Eri's blows raining down on him.

"Under his helmet." Ilia brought her sword up and shifted into the middle guard. "His gorget is small and weak there."

She darted forwards through the grasses and swung her sword at the knight. The black sword parried her first few blows. Ilia circled him, feinting attacks. She held his eye contact. Ilia darted sideways again, turning him around.

"Ugh." The knight staggered, blood dripping from his jaw. The liquid oozed red and black.

Ilia slashed down hard against his knee, her sword embedding in the armour. Blood flowed and dropped into the grasses.

"Ah!" Ilia jolted as something wrapped around her and pulled her up into the sky. The wind buffeted her. The ground grew distant below her as she rose.

Her armour kept her from being crushed, but she still felt the squeeze. Talons gripped her firmly. The griffin flew her over the hills and into the forests to the east.

"No, put me down." Ilia wriggled and writhed.

The griffin dropped towards the trees.

Now. I can save you now.

Ilia glanced at the trees whipping past below her. She brought her sword up and slashed at the foot, nicking the thin skin between the toes. The griffin shrieked and let go. Ilia plunged down into the trees, hitting branches as the ground rushed up to meet her.

Everything ached. Her ears rang. The forest swam and churned in her vision. She closed her eyes. Moving hurt. Breathing hurt. She was alive.

She lay still, minutes or hours, she wasn't sure. What happened? She opened her eyes. The forest wasn't moving.

That was a great start. She took a slow breath. Her muscles still ached, and she had bruises that would make even Master Silvan shake her head, but nothing felt broken, and she could breathe.

Ilia rolled to her side. The bushes collapsed under her. Her arm ached when she landed on it. Still, her armour worked. She was unbroken. Ilia rolled herself onto her back on the protruding tree roots beneath her.

The forest was different. There were evergreen trees here, as well as the deciduous trees she was used to. Where was she? East, but how far? Where were the others? Was Eri okay? There was fire, she remembered the flames, but not anything after that for them.

She pressed herself upright. The world shifted and tilted, and she closed her eyes again, collapsing back on the tree roots. Hopefully, they were alive, and the big knight had more tricks to live. The eggs, though. Where were the eggs?

Ilia felt something inside her shift, like a tugging off in one direction. This way. The eggs are here.

Okay, her friends were gone. They might be dead. She got lost in a forest with nothing but a direction to head in. Black knights were after her, and a griffin kidnapped her. Oh, and the black knights wanted to steal her armour.

They can't steal me. I'm a part of you now. Unlike their armour, we're fully connected. They can't use me.

"They don't seem to know that," Ilia whispered. Her voice trembled. "What now?"

She blinked back her tears. Someone in the court was working with the black knights. Who could she ask for help? Where could she find someone to point her towards a settlement? Were there even outposts this far from the castle? What was one student supposed to do against everything? What hope did she have?

Breathe. Let my power flow through you. Let me heal you. I'm faster than your slow healing spells.

Ilia drew in a slow breath, as deep as she dared. Her ribs still ached, and she bit back the pain. Her armour glowed. A white light surrounded her. The pain eased. Ilia breathed in deeply, filling her lungs fully, and let it out. Her thinking cleared and her head stopped aching. The smell of burning grasses still clung to her.

"I'll do what I can, but this might be too big for me. I don't know what to do."

Feel, the dragon urged. You know where to look. You're not alone, remember?

Ilia closed her eyes and felt the pull inside. West, she needed to go west. How far? "What about the others? I can't leave my friends."

They will find you. He can feel you. You have been connected.

"What?" Ilia shifted to her knees. Right, her master gave him temporary guardianship, and he could sense her through the magic in their neckbands. He knew where she was, like she knew where the eggs were.

Yes, it's the same type of magic. He'll find you. Walk towards the eggs.

She pressed her hands to the soil and eased herself up. Nothing ached or felt weak. Ilia straightened up and took a deep breath. Energy flowed up through the ground and into her. Her connection to the forest was strong.

She couldn't swallow, her throat was so dry. Thank you, armour. Her armour disappeared, but her pack didn't reappear. Right, she lost it in the nest when she tumbled down. No canteen. Ilia felt for water. There, to the southwest, a river flowed through the forest. Ilia turned and headed for the water.

***

The sun warmed her through and sweat beaded on her skin as she heard the water through the trees. The river flowed just ahead, calling to her. Ilia stepped beside the river, wide and clear. A column of smoke rose from the southwest, up in the hills. Her heart skipped a beat. It was so far away.

Beyond the river, Ilia stared across the plains to the hills beyond. She glanced down at the flowing water, rushing fast and smooth past her. She kneeled on the bank and cupped her hands. Ilia scooped up the water and drank her fill. Were her friends alive? She stared at the rising smoke. Please, let them be okay.

She shook her hands dry, a touch of Water Magic helping, and stood. Her fingers brushed over the bracelet. "Thank you for saving me. I appreciate it."

Ilia glanced down at herself. Her clothing was tattered, and the hem was frayed. Dirt coated her robes. She snapped her fingers, and the dirt fell away. Even a basic healer knew all manner of cleaning spells. She closed her eyes and wiggled her fingers, the chant running through her mind as she fixed her tattered robes. The cloth weaved loose ends in and restored itself. Ilia smiled. Being an Earth Mage had some real benefits, especially her being so good with plants. She nodded. Time to get going.

Knight-Master Brannon has good taste in boots. I don't have any blisters or anything. They're so durable and really support the feet well. Of course, with all the walking he seems to do, he'd know what I needed.

Her thoughts wandered to the marketplace. So many people all in one place, all dressed in colourful clothing from their home regions, with many skin tones and hair and eye colours. The knights were diverse like that, but the rest of the castle was not. Why not?

She gathered berries and roots as she wandered. This might not be her forest, but it was still a forest, and she knew plants well. She wouldn't starve. Ilia walked among the trees, following the pull northwest. The shadows lengthened, and the sun descended towards the horizon.

Ilia stopped at a large bush, full of ripe spring berries ready for picking. She plucked some and ate, before collecting more in a cloth for later. With the cloth tied and hanging from her belt, she brushed her hands off and looked around.

A dark shape shifted on the other side of the bush. Ilia froze. The leaves rustled and twigs snapped. An enormous bear stood on his hind legs and peered down at her. He towered over her. What sort of bear was he to be so big and brown? He sniffed the air and stared back at her, balanced on his hind legs.

A breeze blew through the trees and ruffled his fur. He lowered back to his front paws, touching the ground lightly. The bear sat. Ilia watched for a moment as he pulled berries from the bush. No, let him eat. She backed away slowly until he was out of sight.

The forest was alive with animals and the sound of leaves rustling in the breeze. Ilia headed on her path again and listened to the life around her, the call of birds, the deer passing through the bushes, and little mice scurrying through the deadfall. She opened her senses to the forest, both her physical and magical senses. The forest pulsed with life.

I need shelter. Did I learn enough camping for this? The night is warm, so I won't freeze, at least. I wish I had a blanket. Should I start a fire? Can I do that safely?

Her senses alerted her to a sheltered area just ahead and off her path a little. The trees grew thick on two sides and bushed protected another from the breeze. She could snuggle in among the grass and have a comfortable night. If the griffin walked through here, it would never see her.

She walked over and smiled. Yes, this was perfect. Ilia crawled onto the grass and lay back, her head on the soft grass. Her eyes closed and Ilia let out a sigh.

"Argh!"

Ilia bolted upright, her heart hammering. Her eyes snapped open. Something sped through the trees, snapping leaves and branches. It crashed into some bushes over there. She stared in that direction. Branches still swayed, some broken and dangling by a few wood fibers.

She crept from her hiding place, staying low. Something moved ahead. Ilia rounded a bush, keeping down. She peered through the branches, pulling one aside to see better. The sun was down now, and the moonlight didn't penetrate the forest the same way. What was it?

Someone staggered to their feet. It was a person. They gripped a tree and wobbled, nearly going down again. Their sides heaved, and they gasped for each breath. A heavy plank of wood, maybe a tabletop or something, sat lodged in a bush with one corner embedded in the ground.

"Ilia?" The voice was hoarse and shaky. Still, she knew that voice.

"Champion?" Ilia stepped around her bush and walked over. "What are you doing here? Are you okay?"

"I'm fine." The woman staggered and fell to one knee. "Been hurt worse in training before." Champion Loni looked up and met Ilia's assessing gaze.

"Sure, you have." Ilia kneeled and placed her hands on the Champion's shoulders. She felt the thick leather armour under the woman's cloak. Ilia poured healing energy into her.

"Thanks." Loni took a deep breath and smiled. "I'm glad I found you. I've been looking for hours."

"For me?"

The Champion pulled a coiled belt from her belt pouch. "Master Silvan gave me this to track you with. I told her I was coming to find you and help, and she agreed right away. I would have left earlier, but the King wanted to talk to some of us. Brannon called me not long ago about the griffin and how it flew away with you. I set off as soon as I could."

"They're alive?" Ilia's hand shook as she gripped Loni's shoulders.

Loni smiled. "They're okay. A little charred around the edges, but otherwise unharmed. He's on his way. He doesn't have rapid transport, so I knew I'd get here first, if I could find you."

"On that?" Ilia gestured at the wooden boards, still supported by the bush, and threatening to fall with each sway of the branches in the breeze.

Loni shrugged. "Getting clearance for a carpet would take too long, and I didn't know if you were okay. I made do with what I had."

Ilia grinned. "I'm surprised you lived." She reached up and pulled a leaf from the Champion's dark hair.

"It'll take more than a crash landing to kill me. Now, let's get a camp set up. They're on their way, so I'll let them know where we are." She pulled a crystal from her pocket. "This doesn't look too bad. We can stay here."

"There's a better shelter just over there." Ilia pointed back the way she came. "I was just settling down to sleep when you arrived."

"Lead on." The Champion climbed to her feet.

CHAPTER 16

TOGETHER AGAIN

I lia led her around the bushes and back to the cozy spot she found.

"This is a good choice, mostly. Plenty of cover and shelter from the wind. I think the bear who lives here might object, though." Loni pointed at tufts of dark hair caught in the branches.

"Bear?" Was it the huge one from earlier? Ilia shivered.

"This one is a good size, based on these claw marks." Loni reached up to touch the gouges in a thick tree. "Perhaps we should move on and find a new site, farther away."

"Good idea." Ilia glanced around, peering through the dark bushes. No bear-shaped shadows moved, but she didn't see it last time until it was almost too late. Ilia shifted from foot to foot.

"Come." Loni turned and started walking.

"The eggs are this way." Ilia pointed northwest.

"Our friends are this way." Loni pointed west. "If we're going against griffins, I want friends I can trust to guard our backs."

Ilia stood frozen, torn. She had a point. Help is better, but how long did they have? What should she do? She balled her hands into fists and glanced between the two directions.

Loni's firm hand rested on her shoulder, pulling her from her thoughts. "I understand. We can achieve more together than we can alone, though. Let's give our friends a chance to catch up, and we'll save the world after that, okay?"

Ilia smiled shakily. How could she be so confident and in control? "Okay."

Loni linked her arm in Ilia's and walked the girl through the trees. She held a crystal up in her open palm. The crystal glowed bright orange.

"Loni, did you find her?"

Ilia raised an eyebrow. Knight-Master Brannon's voice shook.

"I did. She's fine. We're heading along this path, looking for a good campsite. We'll wait there."

"We're on our way."

Loni closed her fingers over the crystal, and it stopped glowing. "There. They'll catch up. Once we're all rested, we can go get those eggs."

Ilia smiled. Maybe there was still hope, after all. She walked arm in arm with the Champion, weaving their way among the trees. Her legs felt like iron, and she was ready to drop, but Ilia focused on her feet and not tripping on tree roots. The moon rose in the sky and some light filtered down through the leaves.

"Here's as good a spot as any," Loni whispered. "We won't risk a fire. The black knights are still out here somewhere."

"They want my armour. They might not know it can't be taken from me." Ilia slumped to the ground and leaned back against a tree.

Loni frowned. "Would you tell me more about how you got it?" She kneeled in front of Ilia and took her hand.

Ilia shared about her encounter with the dragon, how she stood down the knight, and how the armour appeared. She even shared the armour communicating with her and how she promised to go get and protect the eggs. Ilia mentioned the person listening in, and how there may be a traitor on the council or close to the king.

"Even when I get the eggs, I can't take them back. I already know where to hide them." Ilia stared at her boots. "I don't know what to do about the traitor, or if I can do anything."

Loni smiled. "How do you know you can trust me?"

"That's easy. My armour thinks you're okay. You're not a threat to her young." Ilia smiled, though her lips trembled. "It sounds crazy, saying the words out loud like that."

"Where do we take the eggs once we've rescued them?" Loni raised an eyebrow.

Ilia grinned. "South. To the ocean. There's a place set aside for them. I hope we don't have to swim, though."

"I've never seen the Southern Ocean before. This'll be fun."

The Champion tilted her head, her finger pressed to her lips. Ilia listened intently, straining to hear whatever caught the woman's attention. Bushes rustled. Was someone out there? Was it her friends? Loni shifted to her feet, a smooth motion without a sound. She held her hand up, motioning Ilia to stay down. The knight stood and drew her sword.

The bushes rustled, closer this time. Loni disappeared into the bushes. Ilia sat and breathed as quietly as she could. She gripped the grass and soil with her fingers, feeling the strength and solidity of the ground beneath her. Her heart raced. Her palms were damp with sweat, and the dirt clung to her skin.

Ilia curled her legs up. Please, forest, let me hide and go unseen. The shadows deepened around her. Soil mounded up around her a little, the grasses straightening and hiding her. There was no clinking sound, no footsteps. It had to be her friends, right?

Clink. Ilia held her breath. Clink. No way. Not here. Clink. She peered through the bushes and grasses. A glint of blackness, darker than shadows, appeared through the trees. Champion? Where are you? An armored foot, that horrible shimmering black, stepped from between two bushes.

Her heart hammered in her chest. Her fingers touched the bracelet, the smooth dragon scale that gave her hope. Not yet though, or the shine of her own armour might give her away. She slowed her breathing and focused on the knight.

"I can feel you. I know you're here." His voice had that horrible echo from his helmet. He stepped from the bushes fully and drew his sword.

Please, Champion, where are you?

A sword swung down at the knight, the blade glinting in the moonlight. Knight-Master Brannon burst through the bushes and rained a flurry of blows down on the black knight. Metal clashed against dragon scale as the black knight spun and blocked.

The Champion darted out behind the knight and hammered his armour with her sword, smashing it against his helmet again and again. Eri leapt from the bushes and smacked the knight, disorienting him more.

"Now, Ilia," the Champion called.

Ilia ran her fingers over the bracelet. I need you. Her armour snapped into place. She leapt up and drew her sword. The knight spun, ignoring the swords that smacked him hard and jostled him, and raised his sword at Ilia. He raised a hand and began chanting.

The Champion grabbed his wrist and brought her sword hilt down on his hand. The black knight spun towards her and kicked. His foot collided with her side, and she stumbled into the bushes. Knight-Master Brannon roared and grabbed the black helmet, his large gauntlet-covered hands gripping the horns. He pulled the knight over, dumping the man on his back, and sat on his chest.

Ilia darted in; sword aimed at the fleshy bit under the arm. She stabbed the padded armour underneath, and the blade slid into his arm. The knight howled in pain and writhed, but the big knight had him pinned. Eri stepped on the black knight's wrist, and he dropped his sword. Black ooze flowed from the wound. Ilia swallowed and closed her eyes until her stomach settled.

Bury it. Bury his sword now.

Smoke rose from the knight's wound. He lay trembling under the big knight, pinned to the ground.

Ilia focused on the sword and the soil beneath it. She called on the planet and opened a hole. The sword sank into the hole and Ilia covered it. She watched with her powers as the sword sank down, deeper and deeper into the ground. The planet tugged on the sword and Ilia let go of it. It sank below where she could feel, shifting and moving in the soil as something pulled it deeper.

She glanced at the knight. He convulsed. Smoke rose from around his armour. He dissolved into ash, dumping the big knight onto his knees. A breeze flowed past her and picked up the ash, swirling it up and carrying it away into the sky.

"Get away from the armour. I have to bury it," she urged. "It's cursed." She sheathed her sword.

The bushes groaned. Wait, the Champion. Ilia darted over and kneeled beside the woman. Her leg hung at an odd angle. Ilia let her armour disappear, and she placed a bare hand on the woman's forehead. Healing flowed into the Champion, soothing the aches and healing her knee joint.

"You know, most people don't make me heal them twice in one night." Ilia smiled at her. She poured more healing in through her hands.

Loni laughed, groaned, and laughed again. "Hey, it worked. You're safe, he's gone, and you can heal me." Her body relaxed, and she stretched her newly healed leg out, bending it slowly a few times before relaxing again. "That feels better. You're fantastic."

Ilia grinned. "I learned from the best." She rose to her feet. Ilia swayed. She grabbed for a tree.

Eri wrapped an arm around her. "Easy now. Are you okay?"

Loni got to her feet. "She's probably overtired. She was already half-dead on her feet when I found her, and we haven't slept yet."

Eri gathered her into his arms and held her against his chest. He was warm and she could sleep here. Her eyes wanted to slam closed as Eri carried her back over to his master. She noticed the armour sinking into the soil.

"Thank you," she whispered to the big knight.

"You need rest, girl. We'll find a campsite nearby and leave once she's rested."

She closed her eyes. Eri carried her, the rocking of his body with his footsteps lulling her to sleep. Someone wrapped a cloak around her, and they set her on soft grass. Sleep took her.

***

Breakfast smells filled the air. Her stomach growled. Ilia blinked up at the sunlight, giving the leaves above her a greenish glow. She stretched and sat, taking her time. Her body felt sluggish, but not bad, when you considered what happened yesterday.

Eri sat cross-legged, cooking food on a flat rock nearby. The two knights slept, curled up in their cloaks, not moving. She crept to his side and sat, nodding a greeting. Eri turned some rations on the rock and sprinkled a little cinnamon on the hot side.

"They'll wake soon enough," he whispered. "They need sleep, too."

Ilia wrapped the borrowed cloak around herself tighter. She leaned over to a bush just in reach and plucked a few herbs. Ilia righted herself and set them on the warm rock beside the rations. Eri added some berries from his pack. Ilia leaned over the food and inhaled deeply. She smiled.

The big knight sat up and stretched. He nodded to them and glanced over at the Champion. He took his cloak and draped it over her. The big man kneeled beside Eri and collected plates from the pack. Eri divided up the food for everyone and handed one back to his master.

"Thank you. Let her sleep a little longer. She'll need the rest after being healed."

Ilia took the offered plate of berries and rations. The food was cool enough to eat, so she didn't hesitate. The warm travel bread crumbled softly in her mouth, and she chewed on the dried fruit inside. She was just finishing when the Champion finally stirred and rolled over.

"What happened at the nest?" Ilia turned pleading eyes on Eri. Please, answer. She popped a berry into her mouth.

"You remember stabbing that knight?"

Ilia nodded.

"He dissolved like that one last night. The other one was watching, and he took off, disappearing just like that. The nest was kind of on fire, so we risked a speed spell down the mountain and skimmed over the land until we caught up." Eri ran a hand through his hair. "I tell you, flight is fun, in an 'I'm going to die any moment' kind of way. Especially when you're only a few feet off the ground, and every moment you get more tired."

Ilia choked on her berry and coughed until she could breathe again. Her travel before this had always been the same. Stuck in a carriage as they were driven to whoever needed help, reciting healing spells and herbal recipes the entire trip at Master Silvan's prodding. What would flying feel like?

CHAPTER 17

THE GRIFFIN

"Once we're done eating, we go. Ilia, you know the way?" The Champion raised an eyebrow at her.

Ilia nodded and pointed. Her throat still ached from nearly choking. Everyone finished their meals, and Eri cleaned up with his Water Magic. Ilia rolled her borrowed cloak and blankets up and tucked them in the big knight's pack. Once the campsite was clean, they headed into the trees together.

The forest was alive with life this early, animals waking and looking for breakfast, birds flitting about overhead. She smiled at the small fox, peering out at her from under a bush. Did the others notice the animals, too? Nobody mentioned if they did, or maybe they were used to it?

The sun rose higher, and the animals grew quieter. They walked in silence, Ilia behind the Champion, pointing the way, and the other knights behind her. This is way better than the city was. I'll take the birdsong over crowd noises any day. Ilia smiled to herself.

"I hear running water ahead," Eri whispered.

The Champion nodded. "We'll pass beside it soon. With luck, we won't have to cross it."

It was a few more seconds before Ilia heard the water, but as a Water Mage, it was no wonder he sensed the river first. It sounded like a big river, flowing fast. The trees thinned, and the sunlight got stronger, the forest brighter. Ilia smiled again, glad for the feel of sunlight on her skin.

The forest opened to her left, becoming wide grassy banks that lined either side of the wide river. She sighed. They shouldn't have to cross it. Hopefully, it didn't bend around at some point, though. She didn't know any water walking spells yet. There were no rivers big enough to need it near the castle that didn't have bridges.

"Stay vigilant. There's still a black knight and two griffins out there." Knight-Master Brannon's words shattered her calm, sending a frigid chill through her.

Ilia glanced at the sky. Patches of blue peeked through the leaves above her. Her fingers ran along the hem of her sleeves, and she chewed on her lip. No, they wouldn't let her be taken like that again. She was safe, wasn't she?

The Champion kept them just inside the trees as they skirted the grassy riverbanks. Ilia's heart raced. Eri's hand on her shoulder kept her from walking into a tree when she glanced up at the sky again. A flash of gold passed overhead, and Ilia crouched.

"Is it alone?" The Champion drew her sword, her armour appearing, and pulled Ilia deeper into the trees.

The big knight drew his sword, his armour flashing into place. He held a hand up and muttered. "Yes, it is."

The shadow passed over her. The breeze from its wings beat down through the leaves at her. The golden griffin landed on the riverbank. It stared at her with golden eyes. Ilia stood frozen. Something about the griffin pulled at her inside.

Eri stretched his hand out, closed it into a fist, and yanked it back. Water rushed from the river and doused the griffin, soaking the feathers. It flapped its wings and leapt, but the feathers clung together, and the griffin hit the grass.

The big knight held his hand out and mumbled. The soil softened, and the griffin sank to its ankles. Griffins have ankles, right? Focus, she chastised. The griffin screeched and writhed, fighting to free itself, but the soil hardened and held fast.

The Champion approached the griffin, sword out and ready. The big knight followed her. The griffin shook, spraying water over them. It snapped its beak and shrieked at them, its head swiveling between the two knights.

The big knight pulled some rope from his pack. He threw the rope, chanting as it flew at the griffin. The rope slipped over the beak and pulled shut, tying it closed. The griffin thrashed its head and rubbed it against its leg.

The griffin went still, its sides heaving with each breath. Ilia met its eye. Panic ran through her body. The big knight stepped beside the griffin; his sword raised high.

"Wait," Ilia cried. She dashed over and stood between the knight and the griffin; her arms stretched out wide. "Give me a moment. Please."

"What's on your mind, young one?" Loni stepped beside her and placed a hand on Ilia's shoulder. She glanced down at the griffin, still trapped in the soil, the rope around its beak.

"Let me try something. Please." She turned pleading eyes on the big knight.

He frowned. "It's dangerous. We can't allow it to live."

"Please," she whispered.

"Let her try." Loni nodded to Ilia.

The big knight scowled. "Fine. Be quick and don't get yourself killed." He lowered his sword.

Ilia ran her fingers over the bracelet and took a slow breath. Please, protect me if I need you, she pleaded. Ilia turned and stepped closer to the griffin, moving near its shoulder. Ilia reached a hand to its feathered head, which was dropped between its front legs.

"What happened to you?" she whispered.

She stroked the soggy feathers. The griffin fixed its golden eye on her. His beak fought against the tightly wound rope.

"None of that, now. I'm trying to help. Let me in."

Ilia let her magic flow through her hand. She gasped as her healer's sensing spell touched him. His energy was chaotic and disrupted, and his muscles twitched with pain. Something clouded his mind. His nerves tingled and burned.

"What happened to you?" she whispered. "How do you handle all the pain?"

He pressed his beak against the ground. If he could cry, Ilia was sure he'd be sobbing. She poured soothing magic into him, focusing on his nerves first. His body was full of strange magic and energy, but she could move it and get it flowing better with a trick Master Silvan taught her. His breathing eased, his sides stopped heaving, and he stood quietly.

"Now, let's see what that magic around your mind is." She kept her voice calm, just like talking to a hurt child.

"What magic?" Loni kneeled beside her.

"It's here in his mind. It's like a shield, but not." Ilia shifted her hand and made room for the Champion.

Loni reached out and touched his head. The griffin stood quietly, not fighting anymore. Ilia felt for the knight's energy, sensing how she probed the magic.

"Someone put a control enchantment on him. Someone has been using him as a beast of burden. He's intelligent, though."

Images flowed into Ilia's mind. The griffins pressed and fought, pushing their way free of the eggs, seeking to escape the painful curled up position they held. They were older in the next one, flapping their wings and trying to get airborne for the first time. The flapping eased the pain in their muscles. They were older again, and a mage tapped them with a staff. They felt numb, blessedly numb for the first time ever, but their minds were cloudy.

Ilia pressed her hand to her forehead. Her brain ached. Images kept rolling past of his friends slowly dying, feathers falling out as they wasted away, until it was only he and the other griffin left.

Eri wrapped his arm around Ilia and supported her. "Are you okay?"

Ilia rested her head on his shoulder and nodded. "Yes. That was a lot. They made them with magic,. They're not natural. He's in pain all the time from it. The pain killed all the others but the one. Mind Magic enslaved them. I helped with his pain, but I can't take the magic from his mind. I don't know how."

"I do." The Champion placed a hand on either side of the griffin's head. She chanted softly.

The griffin convulsed. Ilia heard the snap as his leg broke. Loni's chanting stopped, and the griffin collapsed to the ground.

"I'm here." Ilia placed both hands on his shoulder and poured healing into him. She set his leg and fixed the bone, easier with it hollow like a bird's bone was.

She gathered a few twigs and bent them into shape, weaving the twigs together. "I need some thread or cord."

Eri dug into his pack and pulled out a sewing kit. Ilia selected some sinew and wrapped the charm with it, holding the twigs permanently. She left long ends and tied these around the griffin's neck. She tapped the completed charm and whispered.

"You can release him now."

The big knight frowned but nodded. The soil shifted and softened. The griffin calmly stepped free. He stretched his head up and opened his wings, moving his body without pain for possibly the first time. Ilia set a hand on his shoulder again and checked him one last time. The charm was working, and his energy was flowing better now.

The griffin pressed his head to her side. Ilia stroked his feathers as the big knight took the ropes from his beak. The griffin closed his eyes and sighed.

"Yes, we'll help your friend, too," she whispered to him, her hand moving slowly over his feathered head.

Images flooded into her brain, a tower among the trees, and the eggs being carried in by mages.

"You know where they are. Can you show me?"

The griffin shook himself off. He stretched like a cat, belly nearly touching the rock and his hindquarters in the air. He straightened up and stretched his head out. The griffin clicked his beak twice. He let out a soft caw and stalked into the trees, his wings folded against his sides.

Ilia followed. She glanced back. The Champion sheathed her sword and started walking. Eri glanced at his master. The big knight shook his head and sheathed his sword. He started following, Eri close beside him.

Champion Loni caught up to Ilia and kept pace beside her. "Are you sure that's a good idea?" She nodded to the griffin.

Ilia nodded. "Absolutely. He's not a bad bird. Cat. Creature. Whatever. He's been mistreated and never should have been made. Deep down, he's like any other intelligent animal. He wants to live free without pain. Can't you say the same thing?"

"I really hope you're right, or he could turn on us all, and we might pay the price."

I hope I'm right, too. I really do. Ilia rubbed her cheek.

The trees thickened, and the shadows grew deeper. How far was it? Ilia knew the direction, but had no idea. Loni stayed beside her, a comforting presence in the shade of the trees. The knights followed behind. Was the Knight-Master upset with her? He hadn't said a word in a while.

A dark shape appeared through the trees, towering over them. She looked up at the massive stone blocks stacked and rising through the trees.

"That's it. We're here," Ilia whispered.

"Eri, guard Ilia. We're going to scout around." The big knight pulled his cloak hood up and his body shimmered. He faded from view.

"Yes, Sir." Eri raised his cloak hood, and he faded.

Ilia blinked. She felt hands on her shoulders and the hood of her robes was lifted and pulled over her head. She glanced down and her body looked transparent.

"It's a spell, silly. If you take your hood off, it'll fade."

She turned to look at Eri, and she could see him again, translucent, but there. The Champion headed into the trees, a ghostly image of her normal solid self. She glanced at the griffin. He shook himself and seemed blurry, like he was there and wasn't there somehow. He lay down in the shadows and almost disappeared.

"Wait for my signal." The big knight turned and followed the Champion.

Ilia sat beside the griffin. He rested his head against her leg, and she stroked his glossy feathers. He was finally dry and looked a lot happier. Well, she thought he did. He was her first griffin, so for all she knew, he was annoyed or something.

The griffin raised his head and stared through the trees. Was he hearing her friends? The black knight? Was his friend nearby? Ilia listened, straining to hear any sound. No clashes of swords, no fireballs being hurled, nothing.

A few heart-stopping minutes later, the bushes rustled. The big knight appeared and waved for them to follow. Eri took her hand and helped her up. Ilia snuck with him, following the big knight to the base of the tower.

"Once we're done eating, we go. Ilia, you know the way?" The Champion raised an eyebrow at her.

Ilia nodded and pointed. Her throat still ached from nearly choking. Everyone finished their meals, and Eri cleaned up with his
Water Magic. Ilia rolled her borrowed cloak and blankets up and tucked them in the big knight's pack. Once the campsite was clean, they headed into the trees together.

The forest was alive with life this early, animals waking and looking for breakfast, birds flitting about overhead. She smiled at
the small fox, peering out at her from under a bush. Did the others notice the animals, too? Nobody mentioned if they did, or maybe they were used to it?

The sun rose higher, and the animals grew quieter. They walked in silence, Ilia behind the Champion, pointing the way, and the
other knights behind her. This is way better than the city was. I'll take the birdsong over crowd noises any day. Ilia smiled to herself.

"I hear running water ahead," Eri whispered.

The Champion nodded. "We'll pass beside it soon. With luck, we won't have to cross it."

It was a few more seconds before Ilia heard the water, but as a Water Mage, it was no wonder he sensed the river first. It sounded
like a big river, flowing fast. The trees thinned, and the sunlight got stronger, the forest brighter. Ilia smiled again, glad for the feel of sunlight on her skin.

The forest opened to her left, becoming wide grassy banks that lined either side of the wide river. She sighed. They shouldn't have
to cross it. Hopefully, it didn't bend around at some point, though. She didn't know any water walking spells yet.

There were no rivers big enough to need it near the castle that didn't have bridges.

"Stay vigilant. There's still a black knight and two griffins out there." Knight-Master Brannon's words shattered her calm, sending a
frigid chill through her.

Ilia glanced at the sky. Patches of blue peeked through the leaves above her. Her fingers ran along the hem of her sleeves, and
she chewed on her lip. No, they wouldn't let her be taken like that again. She was safe, wasn't she?

The Champion kept them just inside the trees as they skirted the grassy riverbanks. Ilia's heart raced. Eri's hand on her shoulder
kept her from walking into a tree when she glanced up at the sky again. A flash of gold passed overhead, and Ilia crouched.

"Is it alone?" The Champion drew her sword, her armour appearing, and pulled Ilia deeper into the trees.

The big knight drew his sword, his armour flashing into place. He held a hand up and muttered. "Yes, it is."

The shadow passed over her. The breeze from its wings beat down through the leaves at her. The golden griffin landed on the riverbank. It stared at her with golden eyes. Ilia stood frozen. Something about the griffin pulled at her inside.

Eri stretched his hand out, closed it into a fist, and yanked it back. Water rushed from the river and doused the griffin, soaking the
feathers. It flapped its wings and leapt, but the feathers clung together, and the griffin hit the grass.

The big knight held his hand out and mumbled. The soil softened, and the griffin sank to its ankles. Griffins have ankles, right?
Focus, she chastised. The griffin screeched and writhed, fighting to free itself, but the soil hardened and held fast.

The Champion approached the griffin, sword out and ready. The big knight followed her. The griffin shook, spraying water over
them. It snapped its beak and shrieked at them, its head swiveling between the two knights.

The big knight pulled some rope from his pack. He threw the rope, chanting as it flew at the griffin. The rope slipped over the beak
and pulled shut, tying it closed. The griffin thrashed its head and rubbed it against its leg.

The griffin went still, its sides heaving with each breath. Ilia met its eye. Panic ran through her body. The big knight stepped
beside the griffin; his sword raised high.

"Wait," Ilia cried. She dashed over and stood between the knight and the griffin; her arms stretched out wide. "Give

me a moment.
Please."

"What's on your mind, young one?" Loni stepped beside
her and placed a hand on Ilia's shoulder. She glanced down
at the griffin,
still trapped in the soil, the rope around its beak.

"Let me try something. Please." She turned pleading eyes
on the big knight.

He frowned. "It's dangerous. We can't allow it to live."

"Please," she whispered.

"Let her try." Loni nodded to Ilia.

The big knight scowled. "Fine. Be quick and don't get
yourself killed." He lowered his sword.

Ilia ran her fingers over the bracelet and took a slow breath.
Please, protect me if I need you, she pleaded. Ilia turned
and stepped
closer to the griffin, moving near its shoulder. Ilia reached
a hand to its feathered head, which was dropped between
its front legs.

"What happened to you?" she whispered.

She stroked the soggy feathers. The griffin fixed its golden
eye on her. His beak fought against the tightly wound
rope.

"None of that, now. I'm trying to help. Let me in."

Ilia let her magic flow through her hand. She gasped as her healer's sensing spell touched him. His energy was chaotic and disrupted, and his muscles twitched with pain. Something clouded his mind. His nerves tingled and burned.

"What happened to you?" she whispered. "How do you handle all the pain?"

He pressed his beak against the ground. If he could cry, Ilia was sure he'd be sobbing. She poured soothing magic into him,
focusing on his nerves first. His body was full of strange magic and energy, but she could move it and get it flowing better with a trick Master Silvan taught her. His breathing eased, his sides stopped heaving, and he stood quietly.

"Now, let's see what that magic around your mind is." She kept her voice calm, just like talking to a hurt child.

"What magic?" Loni kneeled beside her.

"It's here in his mind. It's like a shield, but not." Ilia shifted her hand and made room for the Champion.

Loni reached out and touched his head. The griffin stood quietly, not fighting anymore. Ilia felt for the knight's energy, sensing
how she probed the magic.

"Someone put a control enchantment on him. Someone has been using him as a beast of burden. He's intelligent, though."

Images flowed into Ilia's mind. The griffins pressed and fought, pushing their way free of the eggs, seeking to escape the painful curled up position they held. They were older in the next one, flapping their wings and trying to get airborne for the first time. The flapping eased the pain in their muscles. They were older again, and a mage tapped them with a staff. They felt numb, blessedly numb for the first time ever, but their minds were cloudy.

Ilia pressed her hand to her forehead. Her brain ached. Images kept rolling past of his friends slowly dying, feathers falling
out as they wasted away, until it was only he and the other griffin left.

Eri wrapped his arm around Ilia and supported her. "Are you okay?"

Ilia rested her head on his shoulder and nodded. "Yes. That was a lot. They made them with magic,. They're not natural. He's in pain
all the time from it. The pain killed all the others but the one. Mind Magic enslaved them. I helped with his pain, but I can't take the magic from his mind. I don't know how."

"I do." The Champion placed a hand on either side of the griffin's head. She chanted softly.

The griffin convulsed. Ilia heard the snap as his leg broke. Loni's chanting stopped, and the griffin collapsed to the ground.

"I'm here." Ilia placed both hands on his shoulder and poured healing into him. She set his leg and fixed the bone, easier with it
hollow like a bird's bone was.

She gathered a few twigs and bent them into shape, weaving the twigs together. "I need some thread or cord."

Eri dug into his pack and pulled out a sewing kit. Ilia selected some sinew and wrapped the charm with it, holding the twigs
permanently. She left long ends and tied these around the griffin's neck. She tapped the completed charm and whispered.

"You can release him now."

The big knight frowned but nodded. The soil shifted and softened. The griffin calmly stepped free. He stretched his head up and
opened his wings, moving his body without pain for possibly the first time. Ilia set a hand on his shoulder again and checked him one last time. The charm was working, and his energy was flowing better now.

The griffin pressed his head to her side. Ilia stroked his feathers as the big knight took the ropes from his beak. The

griffin closed
his eyes and sighed.

"Yes, we'll help your friend, too," she whispered to him,
her hand moving slowly over his feathered head.

Images flooded into her brain, a tower among the trees,
and the eggs being carried in by mages.

"You know where they are. Can you show me?"

The griffin shook himself off. He stretched like a cat, belly
nearly touching the rock and his hindquarters in the air.
He
straightened up and stretched his head out. The griffin
clicked his beak twice. He let out a soft caw and stalked
into the trees, his wings folded against his sides.

Ilia followed. She glanced back. The Champion sheathed
her sword and started walking. Eri glanced at his master.
The big knight shook his head and sheathed his sword. He
started following, Eri close beside him.

Champion Loni caught up to Ilia and kept pace beside
her. "Are you sure that's a good idea?" She nodded to the
griffin.

Ilia nodded. "Absolutely. He's not a bad bird. Cat. Creature. Whatever. He's been mistreated and never should
have been made. Deep down, he's like any other intelligent
animal. He wants to live free without pain. Can't you say
the same thing?"

"I really hope you're right, or he could turn on us all, and we might pay the price."

I hope I'm right, too. I really do. Ilia rubbed her cheek.

The trees thickened, and the shadows grew deeper. How far was it? Ilia knew the direction, but had no idea. Loni stayed beside her, a comforting presence in the shade of the trees. The knights followed behind. Was the Knight-Master upset with her? He hadn't said a word in a while.

A dark shape appeared through the trees, towering over them. She looked up at the massive stone blocks stacked and rising through the trees.

"That's it. We're here," Ilia whispered.

"Eri, guard Ilia. We're going to scout around." The big knight pulled his cloak hood up and his body shimmered. He faded from view.

"Yes, Sir." Eri raised his cloak hood, and he faded.

Ilia blinked. She felt hands on her shoulders and the hood of her robes was lifted and pulled over her head. She glanced down and her body looked transparent.

"It's a spell, silly. If you take your hood off, it'll fade."

She turned to look at Eri, and she could see him again, translucent, but there. The Champion headed into the trees, a ghostly
image of her normal solid self. She glanced at the griffin.

He shook himself and seemed blurry, like he was there and wasn't there somehow. He lay down in the shadows and almost disappeared.

"Wait for my signal." The big knight turned and followed the Champion.

Ilia sat beside the griffin. He rested his head against her leg, and she stroked his glossy feathers. He was finally dry and looked a lot happier. Well, she thought he did. He was her first griffin, so for all she knew, he was annoyed or something.

The griffin raised his head and stared through the trees. Was he hearing her friends? The black knight? Was his friend nearby?
Ilia listened, straining to hear any sound. No clashes of swords, no fireballs being hurled, nothing.

A few heart-stopping minutes later, the bushes rustled. The big knight appeared and waved for them to follow. Eri took her hand and helped her up. Ilia snuck with him, following the big knight to the base of the tower.

CHAPTER 18

THE TOWER

T he Champion waited at a thick wooden door. It was open a crack, and inside was pitch dark. She swung the door open wide enough to slip through. The big knight followed. Eri nudged Ilia gently, and she angled herself through the opening. Eri followed behind her.

Light flared, and Ilia covered her eyes. She blinked furiously as her eyes watered. The light hovered over the big knight's shoulder, following him as he walked around the space. There was a table and chairs, and a hearth. Embers still smoldered in the hearth. A cup of tea sat on the table next to a partially eaten sandwich.

"There's no sign of anyone," the Champion whispered. "They haven't been gone long, though."

Ilia peered up the spiraling stone staircase around the edge of the tower. Weren't there any windows at all? No mage-light lamps or anything?

The big knight took the lead, his light illuminating the stairs for them. Eri took Ilia's hand and followed, keeping her beside him. The Champion kept rear guard, her sword drawn and a spell on her fingertips.

Their breathing echoed in the stone stairway. She brushed a hand over the cool stone wall. Her heart pounded in her chest. What lurked in the gloom above? Would they leave the eggs unguarded, or was someone lying in wait for them?

They stepped around the stone wall and into another room. This one had beds and chairs with cushions for relaxing. Wardrobes stood against one wall. Rough-spun carpets cushioned the stone floor. She spun at a motion behind her. Her shadow flickered against the wall. Ilia pressed her hand to her heart and let out a breath.

"Get them."

Men leapt from the wardrobes and under the beds, knives and swords drawn. Ilia's armour snapped in place, her sword at her side. She drew it and thrust it out into a man charging at her. His eyes widened, and he fell to the floor. She tightened her grip as her sword slid free.

"Good catch." The Champion spun past her, thrusting her sword into another mage. "Now, focus on the battle. We'll talk about this after."

Battle, right. Her eyes dropped to the man on the floor. Metal clashed against metal around her. Ilia barely heard it. Flickers of movement happened around her. A fireball sped past, the heat making her flinch. Ilia ducked as it spattered against the wall behind her.

"Come on." Eri grabbed her hand and pulled her down the stairs.

She stumbled down the steps after him, at the mercy of his powerful grip. He stopped at the bottom and pulled her around the wall. Eri held her under his arm, his sword out, and pointed at the stairs. Light flashed against the wall. Heat flowed down from a deflected fireball.

Silence. No more light flashes, no yelling, no clashing metal. Ilia tightened her fingers around her sword hilt. Her palms sweat. A light shone down from above, and two shadows approached the stairs. Who did they belong to, though? Eri tensed, his sword unsteady.

"We're fine. Come on up."

Ilia knew that deep voice. She grinned. Her knees shook. Did she have to go up there?

"How are you both?"

"We're unhurt," Eri called back.

He sheathed his sword and wrapped an arm around Ilia. She fumbled and dropped her sword. She gripped his tunic as her legs gave out.

"We'll be a moment," Eri called. He lowered her to the stone and shifted her back to the wall.

Footsteps echoed down the stairs. The light appeared, slowly brightening their hiding space as the knights approached.

A familiar warm hand unfastened Ilia's helmet, the fingers brushing against her chin. "Ilia."

She looked up and saw the shining eyes of the Champion.

"You're safe. You can take your armour off." The Champion slipped the helmet from Ilia's head. She pressed a hot hand against Ilia's cheek.

Ilia stared down at herself. Her iridescent armour glimmered and shone in the mage-light. Right, she was safe. Except he wasn't. He lay on the floor, never to get up, and all because of her. Healers protect people, they don't take lives.

"Ilia, even healers should protect themselves. If you die, what happens to all the people you might have helped? So many people who will live long and healthy lives, because you defended yourself. He was going to take that from you."

Ilia nodded, her movements shaky and rough.

Eri kneeled beside her. He took her hands and held them. "You're okay. You value life, which is good. Be calm for now. We'll feel it all later, when you're ready."

Magic flowed into her through her hands. Her emotions calmed. Her heart slowed. She could breathe again. Ilia sighed. Peace settled over her body, her muscles relaxing. The trembling stopped.

The Champion took a cloth from the table and cleaned Ilia's sword. She guided the sword back into the scabbard and took Ilia's hand. Ilia's armour shimmered and faded, leaving her in her robes again.

"Now, how do you feel?" Eri brushed the hair back from her forehead and tucked a strand behind her ear.

"Better. Emotion Magic?"

Eri smiled. "Water Mage gift. You may bleed out while I try to help, but if you're suffering from battle fatigue, I'm your man."

We have to check on my children, her armour whispered. Please.

Ilia glanced up at the ceiling above her. She didn't want to go up there, but a promise was a promise. She clung to Eri and pulled herself to her feet. Her legs held her. At least her body listened and was strong again.

"Come. We'll go past that floor, and you don't have to look at it. Keep your eyes on me. Ready?" The Champion raised an eyebrow.

Ilia nodded. Eri gave her hand a squeeze, and she squeezed his hand lightly in return. The Champion headed up the stairs at a slow and steady pace. Eri walked beside Ilia, keeping her against the outside wall. It was a snug fit, and if he was as big as his master, there wouldn't be room, but Ilia didn't mind the tight fit. The big knight was behind her, and he could handle anything behind them.

She sighed as they climbed past the second level and headed up to the last floor. The top had a landing big enough for two people. She and Eri waited on the top step as the Champion cast some spells. She nodded and grabbed the handle. The door creaked as it swung open.

Ilia held her breath as the Champion slipped through the door, into the darkness beyond. She strained to hear anything, but it was silent within. A hand poked out through the door and waved them inside. Eri pulled the door open wider, and Ilia stepped into the darkness.

The light cast moving shadows as the big knight followed them in, his mage-light ball still hovering over his shoulder. This circular room was empty except for something shiny in the middle of the space. A pool of liquid puddled in the center of the floor, with shards and pieces of broken metal floating in it. No, not metal, eggshells. Ilia pressed her hand to her mouth.

She dropped to her knees beside the puddle and picked up a piece of eggshell. Pain shot through her body and the armour howled, vibrating her bones. Ilia squeezed her eyes shut and dropped the eggshell. She pressed her hand to her heart. Her chest ached so badly. Was it possible for a heart to actually break?

"We're too late?" Eri kneeled next to her and wrapped an arm around her.

No, she realized. No, they're not too late. How does she know, though? Ilia touched her bracelet. "This isn't all of them. There's at least one left, maybe more."

"Ilia, are you sure?" The Champion rested a hand on her shoulder.

"I'm certain. I can feel it." She rested her head on Eri's shoulder.

"What's this?" The big knight pulled a piece of parchment from the wall, stuck up with a gummy resin. "Oh, my." He held up the page, and the Champion walked to his side. "We know this writing."

She scanned the parchment. "Everyone in the inner circle knows this writing." She frowned deeply and rubbed her chin.

Ilia stood. "What's wrong?"

Knight-Master Brannon paced, his gaze on the walls. Eri walked over and looked over the Champion's shoulder.

"It was written by the steward and signed by the King." Loni held the parchment out to her.

Ilia took the offered parchment. Flowing curved letters covered the page, beautifully written script in the royal style. "Could you hold still, please? The light keeps moving, and it's hard to read."

The big knight stopped pacing and folded his arms over his chest. Ilia stepped beside him and focused on the page.

Dark Knights,

It has come to my attention that you have acquired dragon eggs. Normally, the penalty for such crimes is death. I am prepared to offer you a reprieve if you bring the dragon eggs to the castle. Send your reply on the return parchment and your decision will be noted immediately. Should you agree, further instructions will be sent by the Royal Steward. Decline my offer and be hunted until the death penalty is carried out.

His Royal Highness,

Delowain Forimal III, High King of Athia

"Wait, what? What does the King want with the eggs?" Ilia glanced up between the Champion and the Knight-master.

The big knight shook his head. He wouldn't meet her gaze.

The Champion took the parchment from Ilia and folded it. She tucked it into her tunic. "The dragon gifted you with armour, right?"

"Well, yes, but the dragon died." Ilia touched her bracelet. She'll never forget that moment, not if she lived a thousand years.

"Imagine if you had captive dragons, raised with humans. Maybe you have a male and female dragon, and they thought of you as their parents. What would happen if you could convince them to sacrifice themselves willingly, giving your knights armour that was nearly unbeatable? You can do this as many generations as you want, as there are no more ancient dragons to teach them the ways of the dragons."

Ilia stared up into Loni's eyes. "But that's—that's exploitation."

"You live a sheltered life in the castle," the big knight whispered. "You don't see how things have changed. You're so young. How could you? It starts small, peoples' rights slipping away. If only the weak and vulnerable are targeted, who's going to complain?"

"I will." Ilia clenched her fists.

Loni smiled. "We will, but the eggs are our priority, are they not? First, we save them. We'll tackle the rest of the world's wrongs after that."

Ilia nodded. She wiped a tear from her cheek. She'd lived her whole life in the castle. Any trips out to other places were short, and she never left Master Silvan's side. How had things changed? What had changed?

"Hey, look at this." Eri picked up another piece of parchment from the floor across the room. "I think we have our traitor."

The Champion took the page. "Our plan is working. Return the eggs to the King, and I'll have them placed for 'care.' Once your pardons are official, we'll take the eggs and return to the stronghold, where we'll continue with our plan. It's signed by Hamilla."

"The Steward." Knight-Master Brannon wrinkled his lip.

"At least we have proof now. We can stop her, right?" Eri folded his arms over his chest.

The big knight nodded slowly.

"What stronghold? Where are they hiding?" Ilia closed her eyes and felt inside. "The eggs are that way." She pointed at a wall. "Without windows, I can't tell what direction it is."

The big knight wrinkled his brow, his eyes distant, like he could see through the wall. "Southeast. There's an old castle near the southern hills, and they might gather there. It's been empty for over a century. It's smaller and was used to defend the area, but we haven't needed it for a while. The country that kept invading had a civil war. They're harmless now."

"That might be it." Loni folded the second parchment and tucked it in her pocket.

"I started getting reports of activity in the area. We were going to let you know and have you check it out when all this happened. It's worth a look."

"Is it far?" Ilia looked up at the big man.

He smiled down at her. "Don't worry. We have a plan."

CHAPTER 19

I PROMISED

I lia squeezed her eyelids shut. The wind buffeted her, even tucked down behind Loni like she was. Her fingers gripped the woven handle so firmly they were white. She could barely hear the flapping wings of the griffin flying beside her.

"You're okay." Eri's warm hand rubbed her back. "You won't fall. There are enchantments. Besides, the timing was amazing. Miraculous, even. It must be fate. This is much better than my master's plan."

"I can do with fewer miracles like this." The wind sucked the air from her lungs. Ilia turned her head and curled up behind the Champion, where at least she could breathe. I hope she can fly this thing better than that piece of wood.

The Green Lady arranged it. Your mother. You're not without allies. The dragons are her children, too, remember.

Ilia glanced down at her bracelet. She was not letting go of that handle, no matter what Eri said. The carpet rippled under her, jostling her. How did it even support them all? The carpet sped across the sky, zipping towards the mountains in the southeast, hovering just over the trees a few dozen feet off the ground.

"There." Knight-Master Brannon pointed ahead, slightly to their left. "Three people coming from the trees."

"And one griffin," Eri muttered.

"Ilia, will your friend help us?"

She glanced back at the big knight behind Eri. "Maybe? I can't ask without being in contact, and we're kind of busy." She peered over Loni's shoulder. "Land at the edge of the forest away from them, and I can ask."

"Done." Loni grinned.

The carpet veered, tipping sharply. Ilia whimpered and pressed herself down against the rough wool. Leaves brushed against the bottom of the carpet. They sped to the edge of the forest and skidded down onto the grass. Ilia toppled forward as the Champion tucked and rolled, tossed from the carpet.

Ilia rolled onto her back and took a slow breath. No more carpets. Especially not a carpet from a merchant who just happens to be passing through the woods when they were. Nope, from here on, Ilia was walking.

The griffin rested his beak against her side. She smiled up at him and stroked his sleek head. Images flooded into her mind of him and his friend.

"Will you help?" she whispered.

He cooed and blinked at her. Images filled her mind of her healing him.

"Yes, I'll help her, too." She pressed herself up, sitting slowly. A few new bruises, but nothing she couldn't heal. "He'll help, if we can free and heal his friend."

"Will his friend attack us?" Loni staggered to her feet before dropping to one knee.

"He'll do what he can to keep her focused on him. He thinks he can do it." Ilia rubbed his beak.

"He thinks?" The big knight pushed himself up and stood. He stared at the griffin, holding its eye contact. "If he can keep his friend from attacking, the odds are much better. Eri, you and Loni take on the mages. Ilia and I will deal with the black knight. Remember, the sooner you're done, the sooner you can help us."

"Yes, Master." Eri nodded deeply.

"They have the eggs. We have to protect them. They're the last dragons. I promised." Ilia held her hand to her heart.

Loni set a hand on her shoulder and gave it a squeeze. "We'll do everything we can. Is everyone ready?"

Ilia nodded. Her stomach flopped and rolled. Hopefully, she'd be reoriented by the time they confronted the knight. Eri grinned and nodded. The griffin clicked his beak and flapped his wings.

"Ready. Let's go." The big knight picked up the carpet and shook it free of grass and twigs.

They climbed back on the carpet and Loni guided it a few inches above the grass. The carpet sped off; the griffin was close behind them. Loni pulled her sword, her armour flashing into place around her. She pointed the sword ahead and rushed at the group of mages crossing the grass and heading for the hills.

The griffin ahead turned towards them and shrieked. Ilia winced. So much pain in that call. The mages turned, and the yelling began. The group scrambled and mages raised their hands, spells ready.

A fireball hurled towards them. Knight-Master Brannon stretched his hand out and pointed at it. A shield shimmered in front of them. The fireball bounced off, flames flying in all directions. Eri wrapped his arm around her and pulled her back. She felt the larger arm of the big knight snake around her waist. He leapt from the carpet, Ilia against his side, and landed lightly on the ground. The carpet sped away, Champion Loni and Eri still aboard. The griffin sped ahead towards his friend.

Ilia clung to the big knight as she steadied herself. He pulled her back against his side and pulled his sword. She glanced up.

The black knight stood a couple dozen feet away, his sword drawn. "We've been looking for you." His red eyes fixed on Ilia.

"They failed, and you will, too. You can't have her." The big knight stepped forward and pulled Ilia behind him.

Ilia touched her bracelet. Please, protect me. He's the last one. Her armour closed around her. She pulled her shield around and drew her sword. She could do this. She was ready.

"It works both ways, you know. If I touch her with this blade, she'll feel the same agony they knew before they died. Let her feel what they did when she murdered them." He held his black sword up.

"You won't harm her."

"Who's going to stop me? You? Your sword is useless against my armour. Your blade can't damage me." The black knight charged, sword up and ready.

The big knight raised his shield. Ilia felt him root into the soil with his magic. He pulled power up into his shield. The black sword bounced off the shield, denting the surface. The big knight dodged and struck; sword aimed at the black helmet.

Ilia darted around as they clashed, staying behind the big knight. Allow the shadows to hide me. Let me be hard to see. Let me help. Clouds rolled over the sky, forming from nothing. Shadows covered the plains. Her armour shimmered briefly, before dimming to a dark grey. She crouched and watched. An opening will happen. Look for it, she reminded herself.

The big knight rained blows down on the black knight, his shield deflecting blows with a solid thud each time. Ilia darted around, staying away from the swinging swords. She got behind the black knight and crouched. Ilia raised her shield and charged; her sword pointed between two plates in his leg armour. He stepped back and her sword smashed into the plate armour. Shock jolted up her arm from the force. Her hand was numb. Her sword bit into the armour, but not deep enough.

He roared and spun, sword swinging down at her. Ilia raised her shield and stepped closer, pushing the pointy bottom against his chest. She rooted and pushed, shoving hard. He stumbled back towards the big knight, who smacked him hard across the helmet.

A burst of colour rushed past. Loni flew the carpet into him, sending the black knight flying. She spun around and charged back. Ilia darted to the black knight, searching for him in the long grass. The knight staggered to his feet. The big knight rushed past her and raised his shield.

The grass started burning, flames licking up around the black knight, speeding towards her. Loni zipped past and grabbed Ilia, dumping her on the carpet, before turning and speeding back. Ilia tumbled backwards but hit an invisible barrier at the edge of the rug.

Water poured from the clouds down onto the grass fire. The soil turned to mud. The knights slipped as they feinted and dodged, slashing and lunging at each other.

Loni sped around the black knight, pivoting. Ilia reached out and stabbed at his neck. She hit his helmet, her sword catching among the dragon-bone horns. She gripped her sword with all her might as the carpet sped past, pulling the knight from his feet. His helmet slid loose from her sword, and he landed in the mud on his back. The big knight leapt on him and pinned him down.

Loni swung back around, and Ilia leapt down beside the knights. The big knight had his sword arm pinned. The Black Knight's other arm remained strapped to the shield, stuck under his body. The black knight was defenseless. Knight-Master Brannon had a knee on the black shield, holding it down, and was sitting on the man.

"Are you going to kill me, girl?" His red eyes held her gaze. "Do you have the guts to strike a man when he's defenseless?"

Ilia shook her head. "I'm not going to kill you. I'm going to take your armour and send it back where it belongs." She sheathed her sword and let her armour fade away.

"That will kill me as sure as if you ran me through. You're just as guilty of my death." He coughed and closed his eyes.

"Sometimes people die. Healers learn that early. If you don't survive, I'll know I did what I could, but it's not my choices that led you here." She kneeled beside the knight.

The carpet rippled as it settled on the grass beside her. Loni stepped off. "You're sure this is what you want?"

Ilia sighed. "If we leave him in his armour, he keeps the dragon's powers. If we send it back to the soil, the planet will reabsorb it instead. He might die, but he'll be a person again, either way."

Not quite, the little voice whispered in her mind. He's been changed. He's as tied to his armour as you are to me.

Ilia pressed her hand to her heart. "What should I do?" she whispered.

Do what feels right. He can't be left like this. He'll keep hurting others, driven by the rage in the armour from being murdered.

She reached for his helmet and unfastened the strap. Ilia slid the helmet from his head. She wrinkled her nose. A dirty, rough face with stubble over his chin stared back at her. The black knight grimaced and tried to curl up.

Ilia lay a hand on his sweaty forehead. She poured healing into him. His energy was leaking out, flowing to the helmet laying in the mud beside him. She tried to cut the flow, used every spell she knew to redirect energy, but all she could do was ease his pain.

"We need to get the rest of this off. It'll hurt, and I'll help as much as I can." She kept her voice soothing. Ilia glanced up at the others. "Help me?"

"No." The knight writhed and fought. "I'd rather die."

The big knight pressed harder and shifted, holding the black knight down.

Ilia held his head still between her palms. "That's crazy talk. Now lay still."

The big knight nodded to Eri. Eri grabbed a foot and Loni unfastened the buckles, removing his armour a piece at a time. Ilia sent more healing energy into him. His energy was still leaking out, but not all of it. She watched with her magical senses.

"Something's happening inside him. He's being drained, but not of everything." Ilia's eyes widened as she felt around his heart.

The knight cried out and tensed. Knight-Master Brannon pressed harder. Ilia shifted and held his head on her knees.

"What's happening?" Loni dropped more armour beside the growing pile on the ground.

"It's like his armour is eating his energy, but not his life energy." Ilia narrowed her eyes and felt inside him again.

"It's tied to my magic." The knight panted. "It's gone now. I'm empty." A tear rolled down his cheek, taking dirt with it. "My magic is gone."

I gifted myself to you. He stole a dragon's life for his armour. His magic is now stored in his armour, and if he removes it, his magic goes with it. He murdered my friend.

Ilia wiped her forehead with her sleeve. "I might need help. I might have overdone it a bit, trying to heal him." She pressed a hand into the mud and leaned on it.

Loni kneeled beside her and wrapped an arm around her. Ilia leaned against her. Her body trembled.

"I got this. How deep?"

Ilia looked up and met the big knight's gaze. "Send it down until you feel the ground pull it deeper. Maybe a couple dozen feet? You'll know it when you feel it."

Eri carried a large box over and set it beside Ilia. She peered over the side. Two eggs sat nestled in straw, shining, iridescent, and intact. Her armour purred, filling her with warmth and relief. Energy flowed into her, enough to stop the shakes.

"Thanks," Ilia whispered.

Eri cupped her shoulder and squeezed. "It's why we came, right? I got your back." He banished his armour and slid his pack to the ground. Eri pulled a canteen out and handed it to Ilia.

She drank greedily, gulping down mouthfuls of cool herb-infused water. Her body perked up and her energy grew. Ilia kept drinking as the canteen kept refilling, tied to whatever water source the knights used. She finally handed it back and placed both palms flat on the ground. Ilia felt the energy of the planet flow up into her.

The armour sank into the soil; the pile disappearing. The big knight kneeled over the man; his eyes closed as he chanted under his breath. The man lay still beneath him, drained and tired, his eyes also closed.

"Thanks for the rain. It really helped," she whispered to Eri.

Eri grinned. "No worries. I was too far to do much else, and you needed me, so I threw everything I had into it. I'm glad you're all safe."

CHAPTER 20

SOMEWHERE SAFE

Ilia snapped her fingers and the mud and dirt fell from her hands and sleeves. She picked up an egg and cradled it in her hands. She pulled it into her lap. It pulsed with life. "I know where I need to go, but have no idea how to get there."

Loni brushed her fingers over the egg. "Where are we going?"

"To the south, there's an island off the coast, through a blizzard that never stops. I need to take the eggs there and seal them in a cave." Ilia set the egg back in the box.

The griffin squawked. Ilia looked over at him. He lay beside his friend in the grass, his wing draped over her.

"You'll fly me?"

The griffin cooed.

Ilia walked over and kneeled beside him. She stroked his sleek feathers. "Can you make it through the blizzard? I don't want you getting hurt."

He cooed again and clicked his beak. Images flashed into her mind.

"He said his friend will carry the other egg bearer once we heal her, too." Ilia glanced back at the others.

"I'll go." Eri stood.

"I'm smaller and lighter. I'll go." Loni got to her feet.

Ilia rubbed the lady griffin's beak. An image of Loni filled her mind. "She'd rather carry you." Ilia nodded to Loni.

Loni joined Ilia beside the griffins. She placed a hand on the griffin's head. "Oh, I see. You are free. Was the mage who enchanted you one of them?" Loni gestured to the mages laying in the grass, unmoving.

The griffin clicked her beak.

"I'll just help with your energy, and you'll be ready to go." Ilia sent healing into the griffin. She nudged the animal's energy, guiding it along the path she wanted. "I'll make you a charm just like his once we're back, okay? This will work for now."

The big knight stood and walked over, leaving the man curled up in the mud. He clasped Loni's hand. "Safe travels. Don't take any foolish risks."

"We'll be fine. I'll call you when we're on our way back."
She smiled up at him. "You be safe, too."

The griffins stood and stretched. They kneeled again and
waited. Ilia picked up an egg and held it to her chest. She
carried it over and eased herself onto the griffin's back.
Eri took a belt from his pack and buckled it around the
griffin's neck loosely for her.

"Thanks." Ilia gripped the belt, the egg tucked in front of
her and between her arms.

Knight-Master Brannon slipped a belt around the other
griffin for the Champion and Loni mounted her griffin.

"We'll be back soon." Loni grinned at the men. "Alright,
Ma'am, whenever you're ready."

The griffins pushed off, leaping into the air. Ilia closed her
eyes and gripped the belt. The powerful wings beat on
either side of her, flapping hard as the ground fell away fast.
He levelled out and his body rocked her gently with each
flap of the wings.

Ilia opened her eyes. They flew side by side a few dozen
feet from the ground. The land sped past below her. She
glanced at the Champion. The woman grinned and looked
around. Ilia glanced down once and blinked hard. She
focused ahead and kept herself low, so the wind didn't
make her eyes water so much.

"This is amazing. I can't believe I'm doing this," Loni called over the wind.

Ilia smiled. She scratched the griffin's neck with her knuckles, her fingers still clenched around the strap. The egg was balanced safely in her lap.

The grasslands gave way to hills covered in dense and low shrubs, which turned to more forest. This forest was evergreen trees, smaller and densely packed in some areas. Snow still rested in some shady areas below. The air turned cooler.

Snow got thicker and turned to ice, stretching out over part of the ocean. A wall of blowing snow swirled around over part of the ocean. Ilia glanced down. The water was choppy and foamy. She stared ahead again, blinking in the cold air. Cotton robes were not enough. She muttered a warming spell and smiled. Ilia could feel her fingers and toes again.

The griffin screeched, the sound piercing the wind. A hole opened in the wall of blowing snow, like a tunnel. Ilia bent low against the griffin and closed her eyes. Wind tugged at her clothing and whipped at her hair.

The wind stopped. Ilia could hear the beating of the wings. She opened her eyes. They were in the tunnel in the storm. Light shone ahead, calling to her. The griffins sped towards it.

The sky opened and Ilia was surrounded by blue again, above and below. The ocean rolled gently. Not a cloud covered the sky within the wall of blowing snow. The raging storm stopped suddenly behind her, like an invisible wall kept it contained or something.

They flew down to an island, green grass surrounding a rocky hill. Wildflowers burst with colour on the small dot of land. The griffin folded his wings and dropped, touching down softly on the grass. He lowered himself to the grass.

"Thank you so much." Ilia stroked his neck. "I'll be back as soon as I can." She tucked the egg in her arm and slid from his back.

Loni rubbed the griffin she rode. The griffin closed her eyes and cooed.

"Thank you, friend. Rest. We'll be back."

Ilia looked over at the rocky hill, a dark opening waiting for her. "We go in there."

"Alright, we can do that." Loni shifted the egg under her arm and headed for the opening.

I wish I had her confidence. Ilia followed, scurrying to catch up. She stopped at the entrance and peered into the darkness. Ilia held a hand up and chanted. A ball of mage-light rose from her palm and hovered beside her.

It had a soft yellow glow, not the harsh white light the Knight-Master used.

"Useful spell, isn't it?" Loni grinned at her.

Ilia smiled. "We use it all the time when tending patients, especially at night. I can change the colour to suit me, too. Leaves my hands free to care for patients."

"Ready?" Loni nodded at the cave.

The tunnel walls were smooth rock, like someone melted them from the cave. She walked beside Loni down the short tunnel, her ball of light glinting on the shining rock. Crystals glowed from within the rock, reflecting her light. She stopped at the entrance to the cavern inside.

The cavern glowed with a light all its own. Grasses covered the soil floor of the cavern, growing bright green and healthy despite the lack of sun. In the middle, a mossy nest waited for her, soft and cushioning with a depression for the eggs. The air was warm in here.

"We leave them here." Ilia nodded to the moss nest. Her voice bounced off the rock walls, echoing around the cavern.

Loni tiptoed across the grass and kneeled beside the moss. She lowered the egg into the nest. Ilia followed. Her boots sank into the soft soil. She placed the egg in the nest, resting against the other one.

"Now what?" Loni whispered.

Ilia watched the eggs. The light shifted and glimmered against their surface. She could almost see them pulsing with the tiny heartbeats inside the eggs. No, she had to be imagining that. Ilia pulled the vial from her robes.

It was time, but what should she do? Ilia held the vial up and stared at the swirling liquid inside. Images filled her mind, flashes that disappeared before she could blink.

"Stand near the wall and wait." Ilia pulled the crystal stopper out, and the cavern filled with the smell of fresh grass after a rain.

Loni moved to the tunnel and leaned against the wall. "Now what?"

"Now we hope I get this right."

Ilia walked around the moss nest, pouring a trickle of the liquid around it as she went. It flowed thick like oil. Ilia watched how full the bottle was and adjusted the stream. At the halfway point, she had half the bottle left. Good, steady hand, now. It's just like dosing a patient. Who'd have thought all those hours practicing dispensing potions would come in handy for something like this? Ilia smiled.

The last of the oily liquid flowed out, closing the circle where she started. The ring of liquid glowed brightly. Ilia held a hand up and shielded her eyes. The light faded to a gentle glow, shifting through all the shades of green she could imagine, and a few more she hadn't thought of.

A shimmering green dome covered the nest now. Sigils and symbols danced across the surface, swirling among the mess of colour. Loni stepped beside her and stretched her hand towards it.

"Don't touch it."

Loni nodded. "I want to scan it."

"You might not want to. It's full of protective magics. I know some of these sigils. That one is a dream sigil. It might implant images in your head that I can't get rid of, and you might never awaken. That one is the symbol for time, and I mean long periods of time."

"Alright, I trust you. Is there anything else we need to do?"

Ilia chewed on her lip. "I don't think so?" Her brow furrowed.

Loni raised her eyebrow. "Let's head back, then."

Ilia held the bottle up and looked at it. It was no longer a clear crystal, but glowed the same swirling green as the barrier. The same sigils and symbols moved over the bottle, a perfect match for the barrier. A rough spot on the bottom caught against her skin. Ilia capped the bottle and turned it over.

Small letters were carved in the bottom of the bottle. Keep it with you. Ilia tucked the bottle back into her pocket. She nodded. Loni followed her from the cavern, back into the sunlight.

The griffins lay together in the grass again, her wing over him this time. They shifted in the grass, ready for the women to mount again. Ilia stepped beside her griffin and rubbed his beak. He rested his head against her side.

"We're done. We can go back now. Thank you," she whispered.

He cooed and clicked his beak. Ilia gave him a few more rubs before moving to his side. She climbed onto his back again and held the belt. Ilia scratched his shoulders where his feathers turned to fur. He raised his beak and cooed.

"Whenever you're ready," Loni announced.

The griffins rose into the air, their wings beating hard. Ilia glanced back. The other griffin was behind her, following closely. The griffin's ribs expanded as he inhaled deeply. Ilia closed her eyes and crouched low. His shriek hit the storm.

The wind hit her, and Ilia tightened her grip on the belt around his neck. She peeked through cracked eyelids as the wind died again. They were flying through the dark tunnel. Her palms sweat. She gripped the belt tighter and closed her eyes again.

"We're out. You can breathe again," Loni called from beside her.

Ilia opened her eyes. The ocean passed under her, dark and rough. They flew on over the dense and snowy forest, past the grassy plains to the eastern forest. More plains dotted with small settlements and farms stood between the eastern forest and the massive central woods. She could even see the special place in the middle from up here, where the trees were old and still vibrant.

"Where are we going?"

Loni pointed ahead. "Home, to the castle. Look."

She peered around the griffin's head. The wind made her eyes water. Ilia blinked and looked again. Banners flapped in the breeze, flying from the lofty stone towers. She could see the massive telescope on the tallest one. As they approached, she could make out the royal crest on the banners decorating the castle. The griffins skimmed low over the trees and landed in the forest beside the river, close to the castle.

Ilia slid to the ground. "Stay hidden, okay? I'll be back as soon as I can." She patted his furry shoulder.

The griffin pressed his head against her and clicked his beak.

"Come. Let's get this over with." Loni slipped from her griffin.

CHAPTER 21

WHAT NOW?

I lia darted beside the Champion as she strode to the castle. She didn't slow down as she crossed the lawns bordering the gate. People scattered from her path as the Champion marched up the main path and through the gate. Knights nodded to her as she burst through the main doors and into the entry hall.

"There you are." The steward bustled over to the Champion's side. "You have an audience with the King. Come." She gestured to the two massive doors ahead.

Loni set a hand on Ilia's shoulder. "I'll handle this. It'll be okay." Her grip on Ilia's shoulder was like iron and her voice was hushed. "I'm going to shield us so they can't read our thoughts."

Ilia nodded. She clearly heard that last statement, though Loni's lips hadn't moved. Magic flowed into her, and Ilia relaxed. The magic wrapped around her brain like a shield. Ilia's forehead itched. She gripped her robes with her hands and resisted the urge to fidget. Nobody needed to know what had just happened.

The smaller door opened, and the Steward led them inside. Ilia moved a little closer to Loni. The room was full of people in fancy robes and stoles that showed their status or position, and everyone stared as they walked straight up the middle towards the King. Ilia glanced up at Loni. The Champion spared her a smile before focusing on the King again.

She stopped below the throne and kneeled. "Highness, we have returned. The Dark Knights have been stopped and the eggs are safe."

"Where are they? Did you bring them here for safekeeping?"

Ilia dropped to her knees beside the Champion and kept her eyes down.

"No, Highness. They are somewhere of the dragon's choosing. We don't know where, just that they are safe. It was important to stop the knights, was it not?" The Champion held the King's gaze.

Ilia risked a glance at the King. His frown was deep, and she wanted to curl up and hide behind Loni.

"Yes, it was. You have done the kingdom a great service. Rest, Champion. You earned it."

"One more thing, Highness. There is a conspirator in the castle who was working with the Dark Knights. I have proof." The Champion reached into her tunic and pulled the parchment out.

"Bring it here." The King held his hand out.

The Champion stood and walked to the throne. She handed him the parchment and stepped back. He unfolded the paper and read, his eyes moving as he scanned the page. Ilia fidgeted, her fingers playing with her robes.

"Guards, arrest Steward Easmar."

"Highness, what?" The Steward backed a few steps.

A knight appeared behind her and took her arms in his hands. "This way, Ma'am."

"I will deal with her. Take the girl and go. I need to speak to the Council." The King waved at the doors.

Loni walked over and took Ilia's hand. Ilia scrambled to her feet and rushed along beside the Champion, not slowing for a moment as they passed through the smaller door.

"Aren't you on the Council?" Ilia whispered.

"Yes. The King is not pleased. He wanted those eggs. You did well to hide them." Her voice was hushed as she marched Ilia from the castle and into the forest. "We need to hide our friends. Any ideas?"

"I have one."

Ilia and Loni whipped around at the voice. Ilia's heart raced. She knew that voice. "Master." She kneeled.

Master Silvan stepped around the bushes hiding the griffins and kneeled beside Ilia. "You've had quite the adventure. A lot has been happening here since you've been gone. Take your friends here and go to the forest in the north. I have a friend there, a Master Herbalist who can continue your education. He'll help. They'll be safe there, too, so far from everyone."

Ilia looked up at her master, tears threatening to fall. "I'll be back as soon as I can."

Master Silvan wrapped her arms around Ilia and hugged tightly. "No. You need to stay away for a while. Learn all you can from him. He'll teach you a lot. They need care, too, and you're all safer away from here. I'll write when it's safe to come back."

Ilia wriggled and wrapped her arms around Master Silvan's neck. "Thanks for everything," she whispered.

***

Ilia eased the book from the shelf. The leather was still pliable, despite its age. She walked to the bed and sank to the soft surface beside the young woman with bright green eyes. She held the book out. "This is that book, from all those years ago."

"How did you get it if you left it behind?"

Ilia smiled. "Eri got it to me. He visited me in the forest, he and Knight-Master Brannon, but that's a tale for another day."

The young woman brushed her fingers over the gold lettering, as Ilia had done all those years ago. No, longer ago than that. Much longer. "Magic didn't disappear, but it changed?" She opened the cover and slowly flipped the pages.

"That's right. Without dragons around to transmute the wild magic of nature, the same magic you and I use, the mages had to change how they worked with magic. It didn't happen right away. The magic took time to fade, but it happened in their lifetimes, Loni and Eri and them. It was the end of the Golden Age, when magic from belief and wishes was enough. Science gave us new opportunities and a new way to tap into magic." Ilia wrapped her bony fingers around Aili's hand.

Aili touched the bracelet on Ilia's wrist, the dragon scales still shining in the mage-light lamps after all this time. "This is why you wear long sleeves and leggings around others, isn't it?"

Ilia nodded, her wild white hair threatening to escape from her brightly coloured headscarf. "They've all forgotten about the tale, and I prefer to keep it that way. I can't swing a sword with the vigor I used to have, and shields are cumbersome."

Aili wrinkled her nose, her eyes distant as she stared at the bookcase full of ancient books, just like the one in her lap. "Is that why you can use charms and others don't? As a Nature Mage, you can still use the magic from the land directly?"

Ilia smiled. "Like all Nature Mages, I can tap into the power directly in the land, the same magic that sustained the dragons, that's found in every living thing. Our friends, nearly all mages, they can't channel it like that. It's too strong, growing constantly with no dragons feeding on it. Only one bloodline has the ability now."

Aili turned a page and stared down at a bright image of a dragon, still vivid after all this time. "It's a good thing I can read Ancient." She grinned. "Will the eggs ever hatch?"

"I don't know." Ilia shrugged. "I will live as long as the eggs survive, and if they hatch, I remain their protector. Maybe when they're old enough, they won't need me anymore. Maybe I won't die until the last dragon does."

Aili flipped another page. A picture of a cluster of eggs nearly glowed with the iridescent ink. "I hope that's not for a long time. I want you around."

Ilia wrapped her arm around Aili. "I love you, too."

SNEAK PEEK - A HEALER'S PROMISE

CONTINUE ILIA'S ADVENTURE IN HER FIRST FULL LENGTH NOVEL, A HEALER'S PROMISE

C hapter 1

"I can't find it anywhere." Ilia popped up from behind the bush. "Do you think this'll even work?"

The griffin clicked his beak and shook himself, his feathers fluffing on his neck and head.

"Well, I'm not. I've only done this once. But I did promise I'd heal her, and I will. I won't let you down."

She wandered among the trees, her gaze on the forest floor. Ilia bent down and picked up a leaf, slender and pointed, crisping as it dried. Her fingers traced the edge of the leaf, stiff already and turning brown. She glanced around. It wasn't fall yet. Why had so many leaves fallen? Was something wrong with her forest?

With the leaf resting along her palm, Ilia raised her hand. She closed her eyes. "Show me the way."

Ilia muttered the spell Knight-Master Brannon taught her on their journey. The leaf rose, hovering an inch over her skin. Ilia opened her eyes and watched the leaf rotate. It wavered for a few moments before pointing steadily to her left.

"That way? Are you sure?" She moved her hand, even spinning on the spot, but the leaf remained pointing to her target.

The griffin nudged her with his beak.

Ilia pushed his beak away. "Okay, let's check it out."

He bent his legs and lowered to the ground. Even laying sternal like that, the griffin could look her in the eye. Ilia wriggled up onto his back, her hand still held out with the leaf showing her the way. She wrapped her free hand around the soft leather belt around his neck.

"You're sure you don't mind the belt? I don't want you to feel collared again." She stroked his sleek feathers with her knuckles.

He chirped, his neck stretched up.

"As long as you're sure. If you change your mind, tell me."

The griffin stood and launched himself into the air, wings stretching as he took flight. Ilia gripped with her hand and legs as tight as she could. Trees sped past, and the wind whipped her face, dislodging her light brown hair from under her headscarf.

He stayed close to the forest canopy, his feet skimming over the leaves. The griffin soared down the embankment, his wings stretched wide as he glided to the forest floor. Her stomach rolled. Ilia pinched her eyes shut. She leaned forward until feathers tickled her face.

She opened her eyes and looked at the leaf, still somehow in her palm. "Left a little."

The griffin bounded between the trees, mighty leaps carrying him forward and jostling her. His sharp claws dug into the soil as he pushed off with another mighty leap.

The leaf spun on her palm. "Here."

Ilia tumbled over his neck and landed on the moss with a grunt. She rolled along the ground and stopped among some ferns. The leaf flew from her palm. Ilia lay sprawled on the ground, her arms and legs stretched out. She closed her eyes and took a few slow breaths.

The hard beak brushed against her cheek. Ilia opened her eyes and peered up at the griffin. He shook himself and nudged her shoulder with his beak. Ilia wrapped an arm around his neck and sat.

"Thanks, but slower, next time?"

He opened his beak and purred, his whole body rumbling as he lay beside her.

She pressed herself upright, bracing on her hands. It was here somewhere, but where? She shuffled around on her knees, staying low as she peeked under the ferns around her.

"There."

Ilia crawled over to the cluster of ferns, ignoring the dirt clinging to her hands and knees. Her leggings grew damp from the soil. She lay on her belly and reached for the orange flowers. Ilia pinched the stalks halfway up, just above some leaves. No need to be greedy. The plant needed the rest to regrow. She smiled and shook the little beetles from the flowers before tucking the herb into her pocket.

"Now, let's get back and see if this helps."

The griffin tilted his head and cooed.

"I know. We'll make her better. It'll be okay."

She scrambled up onto his back, gripping the belt with both hands this time. Ilia crouched low against his neck. The griffin pushed off and leapt into the air, unfolding his wings as he rose above the trees.

Ilia took a deep breath and curled up more as her belly rolled. I need to invent a better potion for motion sickness. Her stomach lurched as he pivoted above the ground.

He skimmed the treetops, staying low. She opened her eyes and straightened up as he soared, his wings outstretched. This part wasn't so bad. He'd never let her fall, and she got to see the world in a way few people ever experienced.

Well, there was that one time she turned into a spirit, but if the fates were kind, she'd never do that again.

Bright green leaves spread out as far as she could see. The massive northern rainforest stretched out in all directions. So many healing herbs grew just down there, just below her. More than anywhere else in Athia.

The ocean wasn't far to the north, a half-day's fly on griffin-back. Once they found the right cure, maybe she'd have time to go see it. Ilia touched her pocket and traced the edges of her notebook with her finger. She'd need to record this herb and where she found it. The notebook held information on all the herbs her Master showed her, all here in this forest.

He folded his wings and sped down among the trees. Ilia closed her eyes against the wind and crouched low. He plunged to the forest floor, dodging thick branches and bursting through leaves. His legs bent as he landed, absorbing the force. He bounded towards the cabin.

The griffin carried her into the clearing. The large cabin sat in the middle, surrounded by tidy herb gardens, all fenced in with charms and spells. Ilia smiled. It was a small hut with a massive workshop attached, and she got to use it every day. If hiding from society meant having access to the best workshop she'd ever seen, then banish her any time.

Ilia slid to the ground. She patted his shoulder, the soft fur warm against her hand. "Thanks. Let's go see her." She unbuckled the belt and removed it from his neck.

He raced around the corner ahead of her. Ilia followed, heading for the small shelter against the back of the workshop.

"How're you feeling today, little miss?" The gruff voice murmured from inside the shelter.

The griffin stood at the open shelter, his head inside. More chirps echoed his little chirps, higher pitched and weaker. She stepped up beside the griffin and rubbed his shoulder.

The lady griffin was curled up on the straw in the shelter, her head in master Nivvan's lap. She reached up and touched beaks with her brother. Her Master stroked the dull feathers on her neck. He touched her paw, where the skin was flaking and red.

"Any improvement?" Ilia kneeled and moved closer. She rubbed the sick griffin's belly through the coarse hair.

"A little. I think we're on the right track." His hands were rough and calloused from work, but gentle as he rubbed the lady griffin's beak. "You are something special, aren't you? I've got her pain under control again. Whatever this is, it's not what you healed her for when you found her."

Ilia sighed. "I know. I just don't know what it is. It's not like I can even feel a sickness within her, either. So, what's causing it? She breathes our air, drinks our water, even eats the same meat he does." Ilia looked at the massive paws of the big griffin beside her and found no trace of redness or irritation.

"She's a magical being. What if the cause of her sickness is also magical?"

She sat in the straw beside them and leaned against the wall. Ilia pulled the small vial from under her robes, hanging around her neck on a thin leather cord. The vial still glowed, though the vial was now empty. The different shades of green twisted and swirled over the surface, creating an ever moving pattern of colour.

Keep it with you. She knew that engraving by heart now. The bottle surface was completely smooth, except for that engraving on the bottom. She turned the bottom to her and rotated it until the writing was right side up.

It's been about a month since her adventure, since she hid the dragon eggs and protected them with the liquid in the vial. Some time soon after that, the lady griffin started having skin issues. Her heart also beat slower than her brother's did. Was that normal, or another sign of the illness?

"Do you suppose they absorb magic like the dragons did, through their skin or something? Might that be why she's ill?"

Her master spread the paws and examined the skin. "Possibly, but that wouldn't explain why she's having trouble now." He stroked her fur along her spine, scratching gently.

The griffin stretched her head and clicked her beak. Her eyes closed, and she leaned into the touch.

"I know. That feels good, doesn't it?" He smiled and kept scratching as she lay her head back in his lap. "It could be related, though, even if we're not sure how yet. I've been seeing more patients complaining of their magic being different, or not working as well. One even told me a rumour that magic was disappearing in the cities."

Ilia rubbed her temples. "But that's impossible. Nature is full of magic. I can feel it running through the land. If anything, it's stronger than before."

Her wrists and ankles warmed. Ilia touched the dragon scale bracelet on her left wrist. It wasn't hot to the touch, but it was warmer than normal.

"I'll prepare the workshop. I found the herb, though not where you thought I would." Ilia unfolded her legs and stood. The straw shifted under her as she stepped from the shelter.

"I'll be in soon. I want to put more ointment on her first."

Ilia headed for the back steps into the workshop. She climbed the solid wooden stairs and opened the door. The workshop was pleasantly cool, with the windows open along the back wall. Long workbenches filled one end of the room. Multiple brewing stations were already set up for her. Two already had cauldrons simmering, each with a potion bubbling within.

She lay the herbs on the central table. "Is there something you want to say to me?" She touched the dragon scale again. Ilia waited for an answer.

Magic has changed, the inner voice whispered.

Ilia smiled. The dragon spirit hadn't spoken to her since she arrived. For a while, Ilia wondered if she had faded or left somehow. She still called the magic armour for her daily sword practice, and it always responded, so she hoped the dragon was still alright.

I'm always with you. I'm a part of you now, and will be until you die. My powers became your powers, though your body is more frail than mine was.

Ilia frowned. "I'm not frail. I'm just not as powerful as you were. How has magic changed? Is that what's affecting her?"

We are all creatures of magic, and our fate is tied to the land. When the mages killed my kind, our death affected the land. Now they must live with the consequences of their actions. You must live or die as well. Magic affects us all.

Ilia rubbed her chin as she stared at the herb. "So, what's happening?"

Magic is changing. I feel it.

"Yes, but changing how?"

I do not know.

Ilia left the herbs on the table and walked down the hall to her room. Her door no longer squeaked, not since she made the silencing potion for it, and it opened smoothly. She wandered across the small room to her bookshelf. Ilia had packed it with books her former master sent her. Where did she put it?

There it was. Ilia grabbed the leather-bound book and sat on the bed. The gold lettering on the cover still shone like new, despite being much older. The book fell open to the page she wanted. She read the paragraph again.

Dragons don't eat people or livestock. In fact, nobody has ever seen a dragon eat at all. Nests are clean, no sign of excrement. They seem to survive on the magic in the land, transforming it and exuding new magic through their skin and scales. Mages have reported magic being more potent when near a dragon. They've observed a fog rising from sleeping dragons when the lighting has been low and from behind, so this theory needs more testing.

The text hadn't changed. She knew it wouldn't, but was this the key for the griffin somehow? Dragons might have lived on magic and breathed it out through their skin. Did it change magic like her lungs changed oxygen into carbon dioxide? If so, what will happen now that there are no more dragons roaming the land? Is something happening to magic?

Yes, the voice whispered.

"And this is making the griffin sick?"

Most likely.

Ilia closed the book and stuffed it back on her bookshelf. "What am I supposed to do, then?"

Honour your promise.

She felt the little vial through her shirt, her fingers tracing it where it hung over her heart. Yes, she promised to look after the griffins, but what if she couldn't? Healers can't cure everything. Sometimes the patient dies, despite a healer's best efforts. No, I made a promise. She won't die. I'll find a way.

Ilia returned to the workshop. Her master was there, his back to her as he stood at the central table. The knife clinked against the cutting board as he prepared the herb. He scraped the chopped herbs into a small pile and set the flowers in a little glass dish.

"Prepare the flowers as an infused oil this time." He pointed the knife at the dish.

She walked over and collected the dish. Ilia carried them to one of the empty brewing stations and snapped her fingers. The firebox ignited, and the flames grew, heating the cauldron above. She checked the water level and nodded.

"What if magic is changing?" Ilia poured the oil into the upper heating pan. She glanced over at him.

SNEAK PEEK - RUNAWAY MAGIC

CHAPTER 1 – TIME TO GO

T he bushes trembled. A thundering rumble drowned out the birds chirping. The herd of wild ponies crashed through the bushes, darting around trees, their small hooves shaking the ground. She clutched her pony's mane, balanced perfectly on the pony's wide back, clinging with her legs as they swerved around the trees and galloped with the herd.

Water splashed, spraying, as the ponies charged through the stream. She laughed. The cool water was refreshing. Her pants soaked through below the knee, and were damp higher up, just like her pony's back. This was freedom.

Nobody expected anything of her out here, and there was no one to disappoint, just her and the ponies.

She turned her face to the sun. The heat felt welcome, and the gentle breeze kept her from feeling hot with the exertion of their run. Her fingers stayed secure in the golden mane, helping her balance as they galloped.

The trees thinned out. She smiled at the wild meadows ahead, bright green in the spring, and dotted with wildflowers every colour of the rainbow. The ponies slowed to a lazy walk, staying among the trees as they skirted the meadow. Her pony snorted and blew hot air from her lungs, cooling herself with each breath.

Ponies ambled along, grazing on the succulent grasses along the meadow's edge. Birds chirped and flitted about above her, searching for nesting materials and food. She watched them dart about. It wouldn't be long, and she'd be watching their offspring taking flight for the first few times, learning to use their wings.

Aili knew the animals of the forest. She grew up playing in these woods, knew its seasons and cycles. She learned which plants were edible and what grew in each month, and how plants changed as winter approached. She saw animals be born, grow old, and die. Out here she felt at home. Out here, she could forget.

She turned her gaze to the undergrowth. The ponies browsed through the grasses at a slow walk. Aili was close to a spot where a particularly rare herb grew. It only grew in the shelter of a certain bush species, where it was protected from the weather and shaded from the hot sun. She slid from her pony and kneeled beside the bush.

Aili slipped the cloth bag from her shoulder. Inside, she selected the sharpened trowel. She dug around the roots, feeling the damp soil cling to her fingers. Ilia would appreciate her efforts. The plant was already in bloom, and they would waste no part of it.

Ilia was a Master Herbalist and had taught Aili how to harvest each herb she needed. Aili knew how to protect each plant, whether to leave roots behind, or how to pick flowers and leaves, and how to make sure the plants would regrow and stay strong.

She pulled a cloth from the bag and wrapped the plants inside. The cloth was spelled to preserve and protect the plants Aili harvested, made by Ilia herself. Aili could flatten these flowers, but she didn't want to crush and damage them.

With the plant collected, she refilled the hole, lightly packing the dirt around the remaining herbs. She wiped her trowel off in the grass and tucked it back in the cloth bag. Aili slung the bag over her shoulder again, leaving it in front of her chest to protect the herbs inside. She walked back to Leya, her pony, and kneeled beside her.

"Time to go back, girl." She patted her pony's neck, the soft hair gleaming in the sunlight. "We'll deliver these first."

Leya bumped Aili's leg with her nose. She blew a soft breath over the girl.

Aili sighed. "I want to stay, too." She ran her fingers through the coarse pale mane. "Let's go. You can have an apple when we get back. Only one, though." Why couldn't she stay here forever?

Leya snorted. She nudged the girl. Aili set her hand on the grass for balance.

"I know. Hurry up, you say." Aili laughed and rose to her feet. "At least you have a reason to go back."

She sprang onto Leya's back, landing gracefully behind her withers. A light squeeze with her legs and Leya walked. The pony headed for the city, a marching walk that covered the ground. Aili was certain she knew the word apple, and a pony always knows where the treats are kept.

The woods were peaceful. Nobody was out here, just her and the animals. Aili looked up through the leaves, smiling at the way the light filtered through, dancing in a speckled pattern on the forest floor. She inhaled deeply. This air didn't smell of people, it carried the scent of plants and damp soil.

City noises slowly replaced the birdsong, at first a distant background noise, growing louder as the pony walked. She left the sound of the breeze rustling leaves behind and passed into the wild fields around the forest. Aili knew where the roads were, even if she didn't use them in the forest. The path back into the city was just up ahead.

The white towers of the Magic University dominated the skyline, standing high above the manor houses and other buildings. Out here, near the edge, she could see the smaller houses and merchant's shops, just visible over the thick stone walls that bordered the city.

Leya slipped in among the traffic, the carts that magically followed merchants, and mages going about their business. Leya grew up here with Aili and knew the way as well as the girl did. Congested city streets didn't bother the pony at all.

Aili steered Leya away from a larger horse ridden by a noble. Leya's pinned ears promised mischief that Aili would rather avoid. Some nobles preferred to ride, her father did, but most residents walked or used the self-propelled carts instead.

She guided her pony by shifting her weight or pressing lightly with her legs, taking Leya down side streets to Ilia's shop. Her hooves clattered on the cobblestones, getting lost in the noise of cartwheels and merchants shouting about their wares.

Stone buildings loomed over her, two and three stories high. Aili kept Leya pointed towards the University, visible from anywhere for a great many miles. She left the shops and merchants behind as she entered the heart of the city.

The lone wooden building was visible up ahead, tucked in among the public buildings. Ilia once explained that wood didn't obstruct magic the way stone could and was better for herbalists to work in. Maybe Ilia was so old that she moved in while this area was still forest, and the city simply grew up around her over the centuries. She had always been here, and nobody remembered a time without her.

Leya turned into the alley and wandered behind the shop. Aili stopped her at the small shed with a feeder for the pony. Aili filled the feeder with some hay Ilia kept there for her. The pony stuffed her nose in and crunched the sweet hay.

"I'll be right back." Aili tied her rope bridle to the shed at the feeder and gave Leya a scratch on the neck.

She stepped from the shed. A little white fence protected the herb garden back here. Aili slipped through the gate and latched it securely behind herself. The paths led between pots and garden beds, bursting with colourful plants and flowers. Most were tempting tasty treats for hungry ponies.

Aili took the short path to the back steps. The inside door was open, only the screen door keeping insects from her shop. Aili opened the door and slipped inside, as quiet as a spirit.

"What has my favourite herb collector brought me today?"

Despite her shaky voice, Ilia still sounded strong. Aili smiled at the cauldrons bubbling with brightly coloured mixtures and the spoons stirring without being supervised. The smell of herbs being crushed in mortars and pestles filled the room, the stone tools lightly clacking as they worked by Ilia's magic.

She stepped through the curtain and into the front shop. Ilia perched on a stool behind the counter. She spread dandelion leaves and roots on the counter in front of her, and Ilia was sorting and bagging them without magic. She looked up and met Aili's gaze.

Ilia beamed at her. "I smell the Balic plant." Her grey eyes sparkled with an energy Aili seldom saw in anyone.

Aili grinned. "The patch is doing well. It was flowering again."

She eased the bag from her shoulder and set it on the counter beside the dandelions. Ilia pulled it closer and opened the bag, her delicate hands steady and strong. Aili waited in silence as Ilia pulled the cloth out and unwrapped the plants. They were nearly perfectly preserved, still a brilliant green with purple flowers, and not crushed.

"You did a great job." Ilia held the flowers to her nose and inhaled. "You're my best harvester. Your ability to find plants at the peak of their potency is like magic."

Aili stared at her shoes. Swallowing felt difficult, like she had a large rock stuck in her throat. "If I had magic like everyone else, I wouldn't be escaping into the forest and collecting herbs. I'd be studying or working and contributing to society."

Ilia slid from the stool and wrapped her bony arms around Aili. Her hug was tight, nearly bone crushing. She squeezed Aili's shoulder with her hand. "There are more kinds of magic than the foolish University

Mages know. What you do for me is every bit as valuable as anything else you might be doing. Do you know how many people I have healed, people sometimes on the verge of death, using these herbs you bring me?"

Aili smiled, ignoring the tears that rolled down her cheeks.

Ilia wiped Aili's tears away. "Here, I made a salve for the ponies. This will heal the skin and stop the itching." She pressed a jar into Aili's hand. "Here's the recipe. You can make this over a campfire in the woods, if you want to try." She tucked a folded paper into Aili's pocket.

"Now, here's a treat for your greedy little friend, who is trying to unlatch my garden gate." Ilia handed Aili a carrot.

Aili dashed through the curtain and darted through the workshop. She nearly flew down the steps and along the path. Her feet skidded to a stop at the gate, which bumped into her legs as it swung in. Aili stared at Leya with narrowed eyes. The pony nudged her hand, lipping at the carrot. Aili laughed at the hot breath blowing over her skin.

"You little sneak." Aili stepped through the gate, pushing Leya back.

She latched the gate behind her, holding the carrot out of reach. Leya followed her back to the shed, her eyes on the orange prize. How did Ilia know? Aili smiled as she broke the carrot into pieces. Ilia always knew somehow.

Leya snatched the carrot from her palm, her agile lips grasping the sweet treat. Could Ilia hear the loud crunching from inside? Aili fed her the carrot piece by piece. She scratched the pony under her mane, letting her finish her treat.

Aili leapt onto Leya's back and picked up the reins. Leya carried her down the alley and back into the street. She headed towards the nearby University, dodging scholars and students. Most manors were just past the school, Aili's family home among them.

Leya marched up to a massive metal gate. The stone wall towered over Aili, hiding her family home behind it. She slipped from Leya's back and pushed. It took little effort to open the gate, the metal hinges noiseless despite the gate's age and weight.

Aili walked Leya down the stone driveway. The large manor house stood ahead of her. The lawn was perfectly manicured. Aili preferred the wild ivy that grew up along the outside walls, climbing for the sun. There was something about it that even the best Earth Mages couldn't fully tame. She glanced at the copper roof, spelled against tarnish or lightning strike.

She turned to the stables and smiled. Board fences surrounded grassy paddocks in front of the stone stable. Aili opened a gate and Leya wandered into a paddock, her nose diving for the grass as Aili shut the gate again.

"Something you want?" Aili smiled at the pony.

Leya raised her head and stared at the girl, her mouth full of grass. She stuck her nose over the top fence board and snorted.

"I'll be right back with that apple. It's not nice to manipulate me with your cuteness." Aili rubbed Leya's cheek.

Leya sighed, blowing a breath over the girl. She closed her eyes and leaned into Aili's touch. Aili gave her golden hair a pat. Time to keep her promise. She turned to the stable and walked to the main door, a skip in her step.

A couple of younger stable hands unloaded hay bales from a massive wagon, levitating them into the nearby storage shed. Aili stopped and watched for a moment. She'd read about the magic they did, learned the theory, but her heart ached to try it.

A snort pulled her from her thoughts. Aili headed inside the stable. She inhaled deeply, taking in the smell of clean horse, fresh hay, and leather. The windows let natural light inside, giving everything a warm glow from the sunlight. Aili wandered down the aisle to the feed room.

Darik stood with his back to her, lifting bags of grain and dumping them into a container spelled against rodents. He slit the bags open with a knife and heaved them up in his arms. Aili often saw him work with no magic at all. Was that why he wasn't bothered by her lack of magic?

He wasn't from the city, but he never told Aili where he grew up, or what he did before coming here. What kind of past did this mysterious man have? All Aili knew was he was like a second father to her, spending time with her as she grew up. Just being around him, even like this, her heart warmed.

Ilia was the other person in her life that worked without magic. She explained once that magic can affect some potions and salves. She mixed them without magic, or with tools that were specially spelled.

"What grand adventures did you two have today?" Darik glanced over as he slit another feed bag open.

"Oh, nothing much. Monsters to slay, treasures to find, the usual." Aili grinned back at him. She pulled the small container from her pocket. "Ilia gave me this. Use it on Linna's skin condition. It'll speed the healing."

Darik took the little jar from her. "As much as you love those stories, you should focus on making a life here in the real world with us. Find your place. You have one, you know."

"This says otherwise." Aili fingered the metal band around her neck, still a dull bronze. "I have no status and no place in a magical world. All I have is my pony." With a trembling hand, Aili grabbed an apple from the bucket and marched from the room.

"You have me."

Aili froze in the doorway, the whisper barely reaching her. She blinked back the tears; her head tipped back so they wouldn't fall. She left without a backwards glance. It hurt to swallow, and she wanted to be in the sunshine.

She took a few slow and deep breaths, slowing her steps as well. Darik had always been there for her, no matter what. When the other kids teased her, Darik would tell her stories and cheer her up. When they wouldn't play with her, he would teach her more about ponies and spend time with her. She hadn't forgotten him, and now he thought she had.

"Here you go." Aili held the apple out in her palm. "Just like I promised."

Leya snatched the apple away and crunched it between her teeth. Aili stayed beside her pony, running her fingers through Leya's pale mane. What should she do now? The kids her age were in magic lessons or out working already, helping society and advancing magical knowledge.

Aili had nothing to contribute. She wiped another tear from her face, another one of many, and surely not her last. Leya rested her head on the fence beside Aili, her nose touching the girl.

She wandered behind the stable, out of sight of the house. The small stack of hay bales still sat there. Darik forbid anyone from moving them. Aili reached beneath the top bale of hay and pulled out the wooden practice sword he kept for her.

This sword was their secret. She ran her fingers along the edge of the wooden blade, nicked and barked up from him sparring with her. He taught her in secret, helping her hone her abilities and polish each movement to perfection. She still felt he was holding back with her, but occasionally she could surprise him now.

Aili felt the wood grain against her palm. He mentioned it was time to get her the next size up, now that she was bigger again, but he was busy with some fencing improvements here. Aili moved to the shade the stable gave, protected from view by the high stone wall and the hay shed.

She stood still, stretched tall, her breathing slowing as she settled her mind. Aili felt the weight of the wooden blade and focused on her surroundings. With an exhale, she raised the sword and stepped, sweeping the blade around her.

Her breathing matched her movements, flowing through the pattern slowly. Breathe in and draw back, step out, and thrust on the exhale. She knew the moves by heart. Aili didn't pause once, didn't falter, and settled back into the quiet stillness that began and ended each form.

The next two forms followed, one after another, with a moment of stillness between. He promised to teach her the fourth form soon, and spar with her more. Aili trembled at the thought. He often had to sneak her sessions in at night, after the workday was done, but he made time for her every day. Aili was a good sneak, and nobody ever noticed the girl with no magic.

She rolled her shoulders, feeling the muscles move freely. Her body felt better after practice, loose and balanced again. It helped her centre her mind and focus on the moment. Aili tucked her sword back in the hay. She felt calm again, ready to face lunch with her family.

Aili stepped around the stable and looked up at the house. Maybe she could go live in the forest and forage for her food. Aili had done that for camping trips, and Darik taught her all about bushcraft. No, her parents loved her and did their best for her, but Aili felt that pit in her stomach every time she came home.

She forced her feet to carry her to the back door. It was the superior looks from the servants, the constant reminder she only had the rights of a small child without magic, that's what she hated the most about being home. Technically, her bronze band meant she needed to listen to anyone with a silver band or higher, which was everyone over five, pretty much. No servant would boss her around for fear of her father, but they all knew they could. Her stomach churned.

The scorching sun had dried her pants already. Nobody would know where she'd been or what she'd been up to. She snuck in through the door. She knew where everyone would be this time of day and could go unnoticed, like a stealthy assassin she once read about in an old storybook.

The back halls and passages were empty. Aili could hear the occasional conversation on the main floor as she headed for the back stairs. Her father's library was nearly as impressive as the one at the University and he allowed students of all levels to come and study here. There were always strangers in the front part of the ground floor. She kept to the private halls, where only their noise could come.

Aili climbed the steep back steps, seeing by the light of small windows spaced far apart. The servants would simply cast a ball of mage-light, which would hover along with them and light their way. Aili didn't need it, though. She knew the way. This was also much simpler than climbing trees.

There was no sound outside the hidden door. Aili stepped into the hallway near the large main staircase. She glanced down at herself. Her pants and shirt were fine for playing in the forest, but her mother would frown if she showed up for a meal like this. Only workers wore pants.

She turned down the hall to the bedrooms, the thick carpet muffling her footsteps. Heavy tapestries gave the hallway some colour and hid the stone walls behind them. Aili crept towards her room at the far end.

A maid's cart sat in the hall just outside her sister's room. The door was cracked open.

"I just think it's a shame that a perfectly healthy young woman has nothing to do all day." Mora's voice carried into the hallway. "She may not be good for anything, but at least she could make herself useful, instead of disappearing all day. She shows up for meals like a boarding house guest."

Aili stood frozen, their words making her chest feel tight. It wasn't her fault she was useless. The best mages, those most revered, worked to make life better for everyone. Aili would never be one of them.

All she could do was read and study theory and science. She knew more about magic than most mages. She just couldn't make any spells work. Aili could never try the spells she had memorized. Sure, she could use science, but that would only take her so far.

"Imagine how her parents must feel. Such a high-status family, and they have an unmarriageable daughter with no future."

Aili growled to herself. She never cared much for Lalu, the head maid. She balled her fists. Her arms shook. No, Aili didn't need to hear anything else. She slunk down the hall to her room at the end, closing the door behind her.

She stared blankly around her room, the conversation still running around her brain. Darik taught her a meditation that helped. She'd try that first. Aili settled on her bed cross-legged and took a deep breath. She focused on her body, on what she felt right now. There was no breeze in the room, and it was comfortably warm. Aili slowed her breathing. Her heart slowed and her muscles relax.

Aili opened her eyes again. Her family would wait for her. She pulled her formal robes from her dresser and changed. Sorry, comfortable clothes. Society calls.

Aili straightened up and held her head high. This was her family home, and she belonged here. Aili swung the door open and stepped into the empty hall. She walked down the hall and to the stairs, mimicking the confidence of a Master Mage.

She passed the stairs and headed down the opposite hall. The first door was the small dining room they used every day. Her parents' voices came from inside, and they hadn't closed the door fully. Aili reached up to push it open.

"Any news about Aili, dear?"

Her fingers trembled at the sound of a sharp breath. Aili rolled her eyes. Her mother was fretting again. She waited, the silence stretching out painfully long.

"I'm exploring a few possibilities."

Aili frowned. He sounded so tired. She hated being a source of stress for him, especially when she enjoyed spending time with him so much.

"I have a friend who will take her on as a maid. I might find her a place at a stable. She's unusually skilled with horses, and she could teach children to ride."

Aili's hand dropped to her side.

"I wish I could do more for her." She almost didn't hear his whisper.

Aili pressed her hand to her chest. Was her heart being crushed, or did it just feel like it? Could words actually wound someone? Aili was the first person born in her country without magic in centuries. Her existence was an embarrassment to her family, especially with her father on the Council of Mages.

No, she had no intention of becoming a maid. Aili was happy to work without magic, and she could do a lot more than clean up after someone. Ilia taught her well. She could study more herbalism or go into the forest and do research. Maids specialized in cleaning magic and decorating. They had a passion for it Aili just didn't share.

Footsteps pulled her from her thoughts. Aili ducked around the corner to the back stairs. Her feet carried her down, out the door, and to the paddocks. She leaned on the paddock fence and watched Leya graze, gasping for breath.

Leya ambled over and pressed her nose against Aili's shoulder. Aili rubbed her smooth and wide forehead. Her muscles relaxed, and Aili smiled sadly.

"Well, Leya, they're deciding my future. I have skills. We can move through a forest and never get lost. I can fix nearly anything with twine from a hay bale, and I can train horses. It's time we make our way in life. We'll choose for ourselves where to go and what to do."

Leya blew a hot breath over her. Aili grinned. Ponies had a simple view of life. All Leya worried about was where the next treat was coming from and where the best grass was.

"Should we spend some time with the wild herd before we settle down somewhere?"

Leya poked her nose through the fence and tugged at Aili's pockets, her lip catching the loose fabric of Aili's robes. Aili laughed and pushed her nose away. She and Leya could do this together, she was certain.

"I'll get you a treat before we go. After that, I need to pack."

The hay wagon was gone, and the yard was empty. Her thoughts turned to Darik. She would miss him so much. Aili blinked back her tears. She could cry later. For now, she needed all her courage. Besides, how could she thank him for everything he ever taught her, everything that would let her thrive in the forest once she left?

Aili slipped quietly into the feed room and snatched an apple from the pile. She ran back out, putting her fear and worry into each step. She could run off her emotions for now.

The apple disappeared from her palm, Leya's whiskers tickling her skin. Aili smiled at the contented crunching sounds, Leya's jaw breaking the apple into pieces and chewing. Leya lifted her lip and stared at Aili, searching the girl for more treats.

"That's all there is for now. I'll be right back."

She darted across the yard and to the back door. Sneaking like a common thief, Aili returned to her room and closed the door. Her parents would have started eating without her. Her sister would be there by now, and she was more interesting. She was a prodigy with Illusion Magic. Nobody would notice Aili's absence for a while.

Aili pulled the rough canvas bag from under her bed. She used it for camping trips, and she already stocked it with essential tools and supplies. She'd need clothes, so Aili grabbed her favourite shirts and pants. No need for robes out there. Her brush and hair ties joined the pile in the bag.

The book Darik gave her on outdoor survival was on her night table. He got it for her ages ago, when he first started taking her into the woods. She added the notes Ilia gave her on herbalism, nearly another book worth of loose pages Aili tied together with string.

Her hand hovered over a picture of her with her parents. Her stomach flopped around. If she tried to say goodbye, they'd keep her from going. Darik or Ilia had spelled her book and notes against tearing and being soiled, but the photo hadn't been. Aili left it on her desk.

She changed back into her forest clothing, a dark green shirt and pants that let her blend into the background. Aili folded her robes and left them on her bed. A last glance around and she checked her bag once more. That should be all she needed.

Aili slung her bag over her shoulder. Time to look ahead now. No going back. Her family was better off without her. Aili crept back down the stairs and out the door. Once she got Leya ready, she would be on her way.

Leya stood at the gate, waiting for her. Aili frowned, her steps slowing as she came around the house. Darik stood beside Leya, saddlebags over his shoulder. Leya leaned into his scratch, her lip curled, and her head stretched out. Aili's saddle and equipment were on the fence, ready to go.

"Darik?" Aili stepped beside him and set her bag down.

"It's time to go, isn't it?" He smiled, but the lines around his eyes tugged at her heart.

Aili opened her mouth and closed it again. It felt hard to breathe. "I think so."

"I packed you some food and supplies for your trip." Darik draped the saddlebags over the paddock fence. "You've never done more than a week, and I didn't want you to forget something important. Where are you going?"

Aili sighed. "I'm not sure. Maybe I'll go where there is no magic, and I can be like everybody else."

"It's a different world out there. You won't find it any friendlier than here. You can always come back, and I'll help you. You're not as alone as you feel right now."

She blinked back her tears and stepped into the paddock. Leya's brushes gave her something else to think about, the smooth wood handles familiar in her hand. She pressed the brushes against the pony, falling into the familiar routine. If Leya was going to carry her any distance, Aili had to be sure she stayed healthy. She wouldn't fail her best friend.

"Thanks for everything," Aili whispered. "I couldn't even try this without everything you taught me."

Darik nodded, his eyes on the ground. He picked up her saddle and set it on Leya. A slight wiggle and the saddle shifted into the right place. Aili fastened the girth and Darik tied the packs behind the saddle, balancing them for Leya's comfort. Too much weight on one side could make Leya sore. Aili slipped Leya's rope bridle over the pony's head.

He held the cheekpieces of her bridle and looked the pony in the eye. "You take care of her. Don't let her get lost."

Aili pressed her hand to her mouth, choking back a sob or a laugh. She wasn't sure which it was, but her throat ached. "I'll miss you, too."

Darik opened his mouth and closed it again. He brushed his hand over his eyes and blinked rapidly. Aili pressed her hand to her heart. She swung herself up into the saddle and picked up the reins. The rope felt soft and light in her hands. She didn't really need the bridle, but Aili didn't want to stand out from other riders on the road.

Darik swung the gate open and stepped aside. "Safe travels."

Aili gave Leya a light squeeze with her legs. The pony strode from the paddock. She rarely got to go out again so quickly. Did Leya know what was going on? Aili didn't look back as she passed through the manor gates, away from her family home and the man who watched over her as she grew up.

DEAR READER,

If you enjoyed my book, please consider leaving a review. It helps other people find my books, so they can enjoy them, too.

You can find more information on all my books at www.aliings.com. Sign up for the newsletter for bonus content and scenes, tips and facts, book information, and more. All subscribers get a copy of An Unusual Child, a collection of scenes from Aili's life, as an ebook.

ABOUT AUTHOR

Ali spends her days with her horses and ponies, dreaming of adventures and magic. She enjoys martial arts, especially swords and edged weapons, though she practices for self-improvement. She also practices meditation, both sitting and moving varieties.

ALSO BY

Forest Guardians

Runaway Magic

Facing the Fire

Healer's Strength

Scout's Honour

Shadow Hunter

The Last Dragon

Apprentice Scout

Chasing Shadows

Legends of the Mountain

Phoenix Rising

Other Books

Rogue Magic